SKY BLUE

SKY BLUE

KAROL WHALEY

I long for sky blue,
but clouds obscure my vision.
Will the sun return?

ISBN: 9781545201459

This book is dedicated to the Lord Jesus Christ and His beloved Japanese.

CHAPTER ONE

"Last call for flight fifty-four to Tokyo Haneda."

Eiko stood up, her palms already sweaty. She blew upward to puff her bangs from her eyes, glad she'd taken the time to have her shoulder-length hair trimmed before leaving for her new life. It was important to make a good first impression.

Quickly, she scanned in all directions, but her mother was nowhere in sight. She'd left ten minutes ago to buy coffee, promising to be right back.

I've been waiting for this day for a long time, she thought, blinking back unbidden tears. *We can't miss this flight!*

It had indeed been a long wait, at least so far as she was concerned. Born in 1971, Eiko had grown up, waiting for the day when she could go to "the big city" to establish herself as an adult. Twenty-two years had passed since then, and though she felt a bit of trepidation at the thought of being on her own, she was still excited at the prospect.

She grabbed her mom's carry-on bag and got in line behind the last few stragglers at the gate. Waiting assistance to board, an older woman pointed to a figure hurrying toward them. "Isn't she with you? I saw you sitting together."

Eiko breathed a sigh of relief as she watched her mother, Etsuko, make her way to the gate, a cup of coffee in each hand. Eiko was oddly surprised to suddenly notice

1

her mother's age, as if she hadn't seen her in a while. But it didn't seem that long ago that Etsuko's neat, upswept gray hair had been as black as her daughter's.

Sadness and concern shone through Etsuko's dark eyes as she hurried toward her daughter, and for a brief moment, Eiko felt a pang of guilt about her decision to leave her family home in Sapporo and move to Tokyo.

"Eiko, I am sorry," her mother said, managing a smile as she handed Eiko her coffee. "It took longer than I thought."

The flight attendant quickly validated their boarding passes, and in a few minutes they were seated, ready for take-off. Eiko reminded herself that in an hour and a half she would be where her heart had been leading her—to the big city and a world of adventure.

A 1993 university graduate, Eiko had begged her parents' permission to move to the main island of Honshu. Only weeks since that graduation and with the promise of a job at a company owned by a relative of her uncle's best friend from college, her dream was about to become a reality.

After an uneventful flight, Eiko's mother stayed in her daughter's apartment for a few days, helping her daughter settle in. She paid the required "key money" and even provided her first six months' rent. Though Eiko objected, her father had insisted. And so the apartment was now officially hers. But then Etsuko was gone, leaving Eiko to begin her new adventure on her own.

Five months had passed since Etsuko had left her daughter in Tokyo, and Eiko was already beginning to feel at home there. She smiled as she stepped out of her apartment into the sunshine and looked up at the beautiful blue, cloudless sky, known as *nihonbare*, or "sky blue."

"Today is a perfect autumn day in Tokyo," she announced aloud, as she headed down the narrow street, watching the people hurry by in each direction, ready to start their day.

Dodging a bicycle rider with his brakes squealing, Eiko quickly shifted two steps to the left to let him pass. After less than half a year in the big city, she was learning how to live and move about by keenly watching others around her.

On this nihonbare morning, the fish market teemed with customers, eager to buy the morning's catch of fresh seafood. "*Ohayou gozaimasu*—good morning," Eiko called out to the friendly fish-market owner, Sakamoto *san*. "It is such a beautiful day, isn't it?"

"It sure is!" Sakamoto responded as he went about his business.

Eiko knew Mr. Sakamoto understood that a short greeting was all she had time for during the week as she headed to work, but on the weekends, when Mr. Sakamoto's sons could cover the shop, she sometimes visited longer. Then she and Mr. Sakamoto shared stories about Hokkaido, where she grew up and where he had spent summers with his grandparents as a little boy.

Eiko thought about her friendship with the Sakamoto family as she waited for her train to arrive at the station. For fifty years, Mr. Sakamoto's father worked faithfully at the fish market until he died; then the responsibility was passed down to his son. They were kind, hard-working people, and Eiko felt lucky to have them as neighbors. Having made such fine friends made her feel like her new life in Tokyo was working out quite well.

Not so at work, however. She was finding it a little harder to make friends in the strict environment, and her sense of loneliness grew each time she arrived at her workplace.

The train doors opened, and Eiko hurried to get her favorite seat in the corner. At the fifth stop, she made her way out onto the crowded platform, up the steps, and through the exit. After a brisk fifteen-minute walk, she arrived at the main doors of her office building. Once inside, she made a dash for the elevator, while glancing at her watch. She hoped she would have time before her workday began to speak to Sayuri, one of the few fellow employees she knew well enough to talk with, about the upcoming company picnic.

Eiko turned on her desk computer and placed her *obentou*, her lunchbox, on the shelf above her desk. She looked across the room to see if Sayuri had already arrived. The young woman's bag was there, and also her scarf, but Sayuri was nowhere to be seen. Eiko decided to try to catch up with her later at morning break time.

Eiko had just begun reading through her office mail when the boss, Mr. Itoh, appeared in the room, with Sayuri standing nearby. As the other workers noticed him, they stood up out of respect. Eiko joined them, waiting for their employer to speak. Long seconds passed in silence, as Eiko began to feel uncomfortable. What could this be about? She thought her boss's weathered face looked more tired than usual. One by one, the employees looked away to give him his privacy.

Mr. Itoh began by clearing his throat. "I have an announcement to make," he said in a somber voice. "Our company will be closed for two days. Do not worry; you will be paid. My wife, Noriko, passed away yesterday. My assistant can give you the details about the wake and funeral. I'm truly sorry for the inconvenience this causes you."

With that, he turned and left. Silently, everyone sat down at their desks. There had been whispers around the office that the boss's wife was very sick, but no one knew how serious it was.

How sad, Eiko thought. She'd heard that the boss's wife was a kind lady and that the Itohs had been married for forty years. Eiko wondered how Mr. Itoh could get along without his wife, who had no doubt served him faithfully. Japanese men his age seldom had experience cooking or doing laundry. She hoped, since he was the company boss, that he would have enough resources to hire someone to do those things for him. *Wealth does have its privileges*, she remembered her mother commenting when her papa had been awarded a promotion at his company.

As Mr. Itoh's announcement faded a bit, Eiko focused on her morning work until she noticed people moving about. Realizing it was break time, she grabbed her favorite teacup from her desk drawer and headed for the small kitchen area. Several coworkers were already pouring themselves a cup of coffee or green tea called *ocha*. Eiko poured her own green tea and accepted an offered *osembe*, a rice cracker that one of the employees had brought back from his vacation to western Japan. The thought crossed her mind that it was pretty much expected that when you go on vacation, you bring back a gift to share with your coworkers, something indigenous to the area visited. Being a new employee with no vacation days earned yet, Eiko was happy she had lots of time to think about her cultural responsibility in that matter.

As break time drew to a close and she left the kitchen, she spotted Sayuri coming her way. "Are you okay?" Eiko inquired. "You weren't at your desk early this morning."

"I was in Mr. Itoh's office," Sayuri explained. "He had some questions he hoped I could answer."

"Questions about work?" Eiko asked, even though she doubted Sayuri would feel comfortable divulging such information.

"It is a long story," Sayuri admitted. "Let us eat lunch together at the neighborhood park, shall we? We can talk then. I will meet you there."

Eiko's heart jumped at the prospect of developing a close friendship with someone from work. Despite her excitement, she was able to finish several more reports at her desk before the chimes at the nearby community center signaled the noon hour. She grabbed her obentou and headed to the local park. A slight breeze blew her dark, shoulder-length hair, as she walked out into the bright sunshine. Around the corner and across the street was a small park, with a few benches and some playground equipment. Several old trees provided shade for those who wanted a little solace from the concrete city.

Eiko thought of all of the beautiful nature on her island of Hokkaido. Within driving distance of her hometown of Sapporo, one could observe beautiful mountains, hot springs, and lakes. As her ancestors had taught her parents, nature was filled with spirits that needed to be honored. Eiko and other *dosanko*—those born in Hokkaido—took pride in their beautiful surroundings, which they believed provided for a more peaceful, healthy lifestyle. In Tokyo, however, Eiko had learned to settle for a view of high-rise buildings, rather than the mountains.

Sayuri had already arrived at their agreed-upon meeting place when Eiko arrived, carrying her lunch. "Sorry to keep you waiting. The lines were long."

Eiko was happy to finally get the opportunity to share a meal with Sayuri. Ever since they met, she had hoped to become friends with the petite woman. Knowing it would take some time, she had been willing to wait. Now she was excited that they had taken this first step.

They ate their lunches in near silence, exchanging only an occasional glance or smile. Each time their eyes met, Eiko was pleasantly surprised to notice the evident kindness in Sayuri's dark eyes.

At last, Eiko began the conversation. "Sayuri, I was hoping you could tell me what to expect at the company picnic coming up this weekend, but now that Mr. Itoh's wife, Noriko san, has passed away, it will be canceled for sure."

Sayuri nodded empathetically. "Yes, it will. Poor Mr. Itoh. He is overcome with his grief and loss. I think he believed his wife would one day recover from the cancer. The truth is, she suffered greatly as it spread throughout her body."

"Did you ever meet her?"

The diminutive young woman nodded again, as she finished off her third slice of *norimaki* sushi. "Yes, I did. She was very kind to me. Meeting her was a blessing in my life."

"How did you happen to meet?" Using her favorite lacquer chopsticks, Eiko took another bite of fried rice.

"It is a long story—too long to tell during lunch. Maybe we can get together again soon." With that, Sayuri carefully prepared her garbage for the trash can and got up to leave. "I have an errand to run. See you back at the office."

Eiko sat for a few more minutes, thinking about Mrs. Itoh's funeral and wondering how many Buddhist priests would be in attendance. She remembered her own grandfather's funeral several years earlier. There were three Buddhist priests, clothed in orange robes, in attendance, and later a huge donation was given to the temple in his name.

Eiko felt certain that the funeral details would display Mr. Itoh's wealth, including the cultural "thank you" gift to the attendees to reciprocate them for their gifts of money to help cover funeral costs. Her mother's advice would be helpful, Eiko decided, and she filed a mental note to call her to see if 5,000 yen—about fifty dollars—would be sufficient in this circumstance.

Back at her desk, she finished up her last report at five o'clock, already looking forward to heading home to relax. Before she left, her supervisor came by and handed her a piece of paper. "Here is the information on the wake and funeral for Mrs. Itoh," she said, then moved on.

Eiko picked up the paper and, without reading it, pushed it down into her bag. *I have until tomorrow evening to find out how to get to the wake. I can ask the Sakamoto family for directions then.*

The next morning, still in her floral pajamas, Eiko poured herself another cup of ocha. She found her handbag in the *genkan,* or entryway, where she left it the night before. Reaching into her bag and pulling out the memo regarding Mrs. Itoh's services, she almost spilled her tea when she saw where the funeral would be held—at the *Baputesuto Kyoukai,* the Baptist Church. Fear of the unknown made her anxious as she wondered what the wake and funeral services would be like in a church. Would her outfit be okay? Did people bring Buddhist money envelopes to a church? Not knowing Sayuri's personal contact information, Eiko decided she would just have to go on her own and experience it for herself.

After getting dressed, she headed out to the fish market to see her friend. As she turned the corner, she saw a crowd of women on the sidewalk trying to get their hands on some fresh salmon Mr. Sakamoto was putting out.

It must be today's bargain. If there is any left after my visit, I will pick up some for dinner. After the last woman made her purchase and turned to walk away, Sakamoto smiled at her. "Eh, Eiko san, so you have come to buy some of my salmon at a good price today."

"I want to buy some, but I also came for a visit." She returned his smile. "How are you today, Sakamoto san? It looks like it is a profitable day for business."

"More profitable than some," Sakamoto agreed.

He motioned for her to use the inside stairway up to their apartment. When the door opened, he called out to his eldest son, "Come mind the store for me. I am going to take a break. Eiko is here for a visit." The young man greeted Eiko warmly as he ran down the stairs to the waiting customers.

"What is new with you?" Sakamoto asked, as they sat down on the *zabuton*, or floor cushions.

"Well, things at work have taken an unexpected turn," Eiko blurted out, as she sat across from him. "Our company boss is grieving the death of his beloved wife. He was very pale and sad when he addressed the workers yesterday. But the most shocking thing is that the wake and funeral are at a Christian church. Have you ever been to one?"

Mr. Sakamoto lifted his heavy, dark brows, already showing signs of gray, much like his hair. "Where? A church? Oh, yes, a handful of times in my youth, while visiting my grandparents in Hokkaido. Overall, it was not a bad experience, but when my parents found out, they told me that if I continued going, I would bring shame to them, so I never went back. Children respected their elders in those days," he explained. He was quiet for a moment then, and Eiko imagined he was pondering his memories.

Mrs. Sakamoto entered the room then, bringing rice balls, called *onigiri*, and ocha. "Please eat," she said graciously.

"These were made this morning with the lucky salmon we have been selling. Good flavor, good bargain, good sales, good profit. Customers are happy, and that brings good luck to us. Today we have good fortune!" She beamed as she arranged the dishes and chopsticks on the low table.

"Thank you, Mrs. Sakamoto," Eiko said, as she picked up a set of chopsticks. "The salmon onigiri looks delicious. I didn't realize I was hungry until now."

Mr. Sakamoto smiled and nodded. "Eiko san, we are happy to share our good fortune with someone who is from Hokkaido. I think Hokkaido's salmon is even tastier than this. Don't you agree?"

Eiko nodded. "This is tasty, but you are right. I believe there is nothing as *oishii*, as delicious, as Hokkaido salmon. My family always looks forward to the salmon run this time of year."

She turned to address Mrs. Sakamoto. "Speaking of families, does anyone in your family happen to know what takes place at a church wake or funeral? My boss's wife just passed away, and the wake is tonight at a Baptist church. I'm a little nervous about going."

"Thankfully, I have never been in a church," Mrs. Sakamoto responded, her passion surprising Eiko. "I have heard Christians do really peculiar things. I do not think it is right for Japanese to get involved in a foreign religion. It only brings shame and misery to the family. Your poor boss! I am sure he has suffered loss in his home and business because of his wife's choices."

"Mama!" Mr. Sakamoto interrupted. "Why are you saying those things? The people I met at church when I was a youth were kind and caring. At Christmas, they gave out sweet treats to everyone who attended—even to all of the guests."

"That is all you remember, isn't it?" his wife teased, her tone softening. "Don't worry, Eiko," she said with a reassuring voice. "There will be more Buddhists in attendance at the church wake than Christians. You can count on it. Now, if you will excuse me for a few minutes, I believe I have an appropriate envelope you can use."

When Eiko was ready to leave, she thanked the Sakamotos for the snack and the envelope, and she apologized for coming at such a busy time. As they returned to the genkan, Mr. Sakamoto reminded her, "You are always welcome in our home. Do not worry about interrupting our day."

"Thank you. I will return again." Eiko closed the door behind her, then made her way through the store and out to the street.

Arriving at home, she laid out her black dress and white pearls to wear to the wake. Then she prepared the traditional money envelope that Japanese take to funerals to help cover the cost. Now she was ready, but she couldn't calm her anxious thoughts. Why did it have to be at a church? She wondered if Mrs. Itoh had been a devout Christian and church member.

After dinner, Eiko rode the crowded train to her destination, then quickly checked the written directions the Sakamotos had given her. Going out the south exit, she walked for two blocks and turned right at the post office. She proceeded past a dry-cleaning shop and a small neighborhood park, where children were playing. About fifteen minutes later, she noticed the road had narrowed, and there were no longer any cars or pedestrians around. According to the directions, she should look for a convenience store, but she didn't see any signs.

It would be nice if the church was located on the main road so people could find it conveniently. They sure do not make it easy for people to come.

Her thoughts were interrupted when she heard her name being called from a distance.

"Eiko *chan*, is that you?" She turned and spotted Satoh from work. He grinned when their eyes met. "Are you as lost as I am?"

She smiled at his boyish good looks. His short hair was swept to one side, and his dark eyes seemed to dance. Satoh had gotten hired at the company the same time she did. They had several conversations during their weeks of training, but were later assigned to different departments.

"Satoh *kun*, I am not sure if I am lost or not. I have not yet decided."

"Well, I came from the other direction and did not find the convenience store. You do not think it is this building right in front of us with the scaffolding and tarps around it, do you?" Satoh walked over and lifted a tarp to peek underneath.

Eiko joined him and spotted an older man, painting near the edge of the roof.

"Is this a convenience store you are working on?" Satoh called out, after catching the man's attention.

"Yes. Why do you ask?"

"We are looking for a church in this neighborhood. The convenience store is our landmark where we need to turn."

The man nodded and pointed. "Yes, yes. I see the church from here on the rooftop. Right over there. Follow the road behind the convenience store for three or four blocks, and the church will be on the left. You will see a small cross on the building."

"Thank you," Eiko said politely, adding a quick bow. "You have helped us more than we thought possible."

Satoh and Eiko followed the workman's directions right to the neighborhood church. Seeing the illuminated cross, Eiko wondered at its significance. Some of her friends had trendy cross jewelry, but none of them went to church. *Maybe it is something I should find out about some day.*

As the two of them entered the church, they removed their shoes and slid their feet into church slippers, placing their shoes on the wooden shelves that lined both sides of the entryway. Once beyond the entryway, they found themselves waiting in a brief line to sign the memorial book and leave their cash envelopes. According to Japanese culture, each person would then receive a thank-you gift from the bereaved family, in appreciation for their support.

Eiko knew that, at Buddhist funerals, the thank-you gift was usually something traditional or useful, such as tea, coffee, sugar, or towels. Satoh accepted his wrapped gift, as Eiko wondered what sort of gift churches might give out.

"Probably propaganda," Satoh said when she asked his opinion on the matter. "Maybe we should just throw it away at home, or I could save mine to donate to my older sister's school bazaar. They have them every year to raise money for unfunded projects."

Eiko nodded but decided she would not throw hers away. She was already curious about what it might be, but she kept that thought to herself.

As they entered the main room, where Eiko assumed the service would take place, she noticed the church was already quite full. She saw many company employees, but she also saw people she didn't recognize. The boss and his family sat up in the first few long benches on the right-hand side.

After Eiko and Satoh had found a seat in the back, an elderly man stood up in the front and introduced himself as the pastor of the church. He welcomed the guests and informed everyone that the wake would begin after a few moments of silence, followed by a prayer.

Eiko's alert eyes searched the room for Sayuri. She spotted her at last, sitting in the row behind the boss's family members. Eiko was thankful for her back-row seat on the left side. She glanced at Satoh and decided he too was thankful, as his eyes were already closed and his head bowed. If they were in the front of the church, everyone would notice him sleeping. She hoped he wouldn't snore.

The pastor looked frail, but when he began to pray, a strong, powerful voice, full of expression and hope, filled the sanctuary. He said he was praying to the merciful heavenly Father, Creator, and Savior of the world. Eiko had no idea who this God was. How could one god be that big? The only gods she knew and respected were those who were known to have powers to comfort Japanese with their unique problems.

As Eiko pondered this difference, she heard the pastor say, "Let us repeat together the Lord's prayer. For those who need the words, they are printed in the program." The church people joined the pastor as he prayed, "Our Father in heaven: May your holy name be honoured; may your Kingdom come; may your will be done on earth as it is in heaven." Eiko noticed the printed prayer was referenced as Matthew 6:9-10, GNB. The prayer continued until Eiko heard "amen" at the end.

She raised her head when she heard music coming from the piano and saw a small choir standing nearby.

They sang, "What a friend we have in Jesus, all our sins and griefs to bear."[i] The song's message was tender—Jesus, a Friend to everyone, desires to carry all of our burdens, as we confess them in prayer. Eiko thought she might like to meet this Jesus someday. She wondered if He had ever visited Japan.

When the wake was over, the church people served tea and delicious osembe to everyone. Eiko felt it was gracious of them to do that, since the guests outnumbered the regular attenders. Eiko imagined she would remember the sweet smiles and kind expressions on the church people's faces for quite a while.

As they left the church and headed for the train station, Eiko tried to get Satoh to talk about the wake, but he didn't seem interested. He said he had a headache, and all he could think about was getting home and going to bed.

Eiko tried to remain silent for a few moments but soon asked, "Satoh kun, do you think we should be afraid of church people? I have heard they live by different rules than we do. An older friend told me that people going to church end up just pretending because they cannot measure up to what is expected of them. What do you think?"

His brow drew together in a frown. "I think all religion is for weak people. I do not need it myself. You do not seem needy to me either, Eiko. I would not give religion or church another thought. It is a waste of time."

Eiko wasn't pleased with his answer and decided to walk the rest of the way in silence, which would probably help his headache anyway. But her mind was busy. *Those people did not seem weak. They seemed happy and peaceful.* She sighed.

---

i   Public Domain.

Hopefully, she would soon have an opportunity to speak to Sayuri and ask her opinions about the church people, since Satoh didn't seem interested.

When the train arrived at her stop, she exited and walked briskly in the cool evening air to her apartment, where she finally had a chance to open the present she had received at the wake. She held the small package and began to pick at one of the pieces of tape stuck on the wrapping paper, but she was interrupted by the ringing of her phone. She slid the package into a drawer of the chest next to her bed so she could answer the call. The gift would have to wait until another day. She was ready to think about something else.

CHAPTER TWO

After taking two days off the previous week, due to the wake and funeral, Eiko was glad to be heading to work on Monday morning. It surprised her how easily she had given in to her desire to sleep away most of her long weekend. Living alone and working for the company was proving more stressful than she realized. But today she felt full of energy and ready for whatever might happen.

She left home a few minutes early, hoping to run into Sayuri before work started. Ever since the wake, Eiko's curiosity had grown about Sayuri's personal connection with the boss's wife. Eiko's morning commute by train and on foot provided her time to think about what she wanted to say to her new friend.

As the office building came into view, Eiko spotted Sayuri and a handful of other workers going through the front entrance. She quickened her pace and managed to catch the same elevator with Sayuri, sliding through the door just before it closed.

"Ohayou gozaimasu," Eiko whispered to Sayuri. Sayuri smiled back and waited for the elevator to stop at their floor before she continued the conversation.

"Did you attend Mrs. Itoh's wake and funeral?" Sayuri asked as they walked toward their desks.

"Only the wake," Eiko confessed. "How did the funeral go the next morning?"

"The church was full again. I think that day was especially meaningful to the church members. Mr. Itoh thanked everyone for their kindness and announced he had purchased a baby grand piano as a present to the church in memory of his wife. There wasn't a dry eye anywhere."

"Wow! Such an extravagant gift. Mr. Itoh must have loved his wife very much."

Sayuri nodded. "Yes. It seems so. Well, I need to get ready for my work day. Talk to you later."

"Would you like to meet me at the park on our lunch break?"

"Okay. I can do that." Sayuri smiled. "See you then."

The office was unusually quiet for a Monday morning; only the hum of the copier could be heard. Everyone had extra work to do because the office had been closed. The employees were feeling sorry for Mr. Itoh and hoped to lift his spirits by catching up on all the missed work, even if it meant staying late. As it turned out, Mr. Itoh had some personal business to attend to and didn't come in to the office at all that day. Rumors circulated that he would be there the next day.

By the time Eiko arrived at the park, she saw that Sayuri was already there, sitting on a bench and waiting for her. Eiko smiled as she approached her new friend.

Sayuri's face lit up, and she called out, "Look at the leaves changing color, Eiko. Creator God made autumn so beautiful in Japan."

Eiko didn't know how to respond to Sayuri's comment, so she smiled as she changed the subject. "Sorry I'm late. I had to wait for the next elevator. Everyone seems to have the same idea about spending time outside today."

Sayuri nodded, as she opened her smoked eel salad. "Yes, indeed. It would be sad to miss such a nice day by staying inside the building."

Eiko sat down beside her and opened her lunch of rice and boiled vegetables. "How are you doing today? With Mrs. Itoh's funeral behind us and all..."

Sayuri paused a minute before answering. "I'm okay. It was hard to say goodbye, but she is in a better place now, even more peaceful than this lovely park."

Eiko wondered what place that might be, then dismissed the thought and instead asked the question that was on her mind. "So, you knew her well?" Before Sayuri could answer, Eiko softened her request. "You don't have to answer such a personal question. I'm sorry."

"No, don't be sorry," Sayuri assured her. "It is a part of my story that I enjoy telling." She took another bite, chewed, and swallowed before continuing. "I met her five years ago, before she got cancer. I was a recipient of her kindness. She was a lovely lady, so sweet and gentle. She was different than everyone else in my life at that time. I will be indebted to her for eternity."

Eiko frowned, curious. "What kindness did she show you? You said it changed your life. I am sorry if I am being rude; I just don't understand what you mean."

"You will understand my story, I am sure, when I can share everything that happened." She paused while packing up what was left of her lunch and placing it in her obentou. "But we must not be tardy getting back from lunch."

Eiko nodded as she watched Sayuri prepare to leave. She especially noticed the pretty fabric of the bag that held her obentou. Luscious purple grapes were attached to branches and hung in clusters on a vine. Below the design were the words, "I am the Vine and you are the branches." Understanding the words but not their meaning, Eiko came to the conclusion that there were lots of things about Sayuri that she couldn't figure out—at least not yet. She hoped that would change as she got to know her better.

Sayuri interrupted Eiko's thoughts. "Can you meet me after work at the coffee shop by the train station? I would like to take time to finish telling you my story."

"Sure," Eiko said, pleased at the offer.

"Good! See you then." Sayuri picked up the lovely cloth bag and pulled the drawstrings together before rising to leave. Eiko did the same.

Once back at her desk, Eiko tried to focus on her work assignments, but her thoughts returned, time and again, to her lunch conversation with Sayuri. Looking forward to their time at the coffee shop after work, she made herself concentrate on her work so she could be sure to get everything done in time.

"Excuse me, Eiko san." A middle-aged woman with graying hair stood beside Eiko's desk and spoke to her in a hesitant voice. "I need to leave work early today, and the supervisor has agreed, as long as you take care of my last two reports. I must clean the grave of my father and prepare for a few family members who are coming. The responsibility falls to me because I am an only child."

Eiko liked the quiet woman, who sat at the desk next to hers. She was a hard worker and never complained about anything. "It is a week ahead of the equinox holiday," Eiko observed. "You are very dedicated to do it now."

"I know. But next week, on the real holiday, we must travel to Sendai to care for the graves of my husband's grandparents. His father is too elderly now to do it."

Eiko thought about her plans after work with Sayuri and how taking on her coworker's assignments might interfere, but something she had learned at the new employee orientation meeting came to mind: *Company workers are on the same team. It is everyone's duty to help the team succeed.*

"Sure, no problem, Akiyama san," she said. "I will finish up your work. Hope everything goes well for you."

The woman bowed humbly, gathered her things, and left.

Eiko looked through the extra work and wondered again if it would make her late for her meeting with Sayuri. She started filling out the requisition forms and filing them in their proper place. She was glad she could work quickly without making mistakes. Her business professor at university had told her she always produced excellent work. Even though Eiko was highly skilled, the professor had warned her that she would be starting at an entry-level job because she was young, and she might be treated differently as a female. She recalled another principle that confirmed this was true, something else she had learned during her company orientation. *Respect those who are older than you and who have been at the company longer than you. They got where they are because of patience and perseverance in the workplace.*

At five o'clock, Eiko had only two more forms to complete. In no time she was reaching for her sweater and bag to head over to the coffee shop. Pleased that all of her desk work—as well as that of her coworker—was finished, she was already looking forward to a cheerful time with Sayuri.

As soon as she opened the door of the little coffee shop, Eiko saw Sayuri nestled in the corner booth with her head bent over an open book. Her stylishly short dark hair shone under the overhead light.

"I hope I did not keep you waiting," Eiko said as she approached the booth, a smile tugging at the corners of her mouth.

Sayuri closed her book and looked up at Eiko's grinning face. "Not at all. But something has you in a good mood."

"Actually, I am in a good mood, eager to hear your story."

Sayuri sobered. "I hope you will not be disappointed. Why don't we order something before I begin?"

Eiko agreed, and they both ordered wheat tea and a tuna sandwich, waiting for the waitress to leave before Sayuri began to speak.

"My story starts off sad, but the ending is happy, so do not feel sorry for me, okay?"

Eiko nodded, looking forward to hearing the rest of Sayuri's story.

"Growing up, I knew my family was somehow different," Sayuri began. "My siblings and I rarely received love or special attention from our parents. They mostly spent time outside the home on their own selfish desires, leaving us to care for ourselves. At our friends' homes, though, we were sometimes able to forget our troubles."

Sayuri paused for a moment, as the waitress brought their tea. "When I got discouraged," she continued, "I would dream of one day belonging to a better family, where I was valued and loved. I am sure my sisters and brother dreamed of the same thing, but we never talked about it. As the oldest child, I tried to watch over my siblings, but I was not able to protect their hearts. Things might have been different if our relatives had not lived so far from us.

"I decided in my heart that I would leave home as soon as I could after high school graduation. I would work until I found a wonderful man to marry, and together we would start our dream family. Sadly, my plans fell apart when I was seventeen."

Eiko took a sip of tea and wondered if she should say something, but before she could decide, Sayuri sighed and went on. "That year I met a young, intelligent boy with a good sense of humor. He treated me with tenderness and had a special way of lifting my spirits. His parents were wealthy, and since he was their only child, they spoiled him with a large monthly allowance to spend as he pleased. We went to movies, ate out, and bought clothes and electronic gadgets—you know, all the things that young people enjoy. I felt valued and loved.

"As a bonus, he seemed to like my siblings. Occasionally he brought each of my sisters and my brother a surprise gift. My parents did not say anything about the new items all of us had, but they did notice my happiness and needled me to find out what was behind it. I told them I had a new friend who was really nice and lots of fun to be with. My mother warned me that if I started to neglect my responsibilities around home, especially regarding my siblings, my new friendship would have to end. She never even bothered to ask if my friend was a girl or a young man. Sadly, she was not interested."

The waitress brought the rest of their order then and placed the bill in the round plastic stand on the edge of the table. Sayuri took a bite of her sandwich and the two of them enjoyed a brief silence as they chewed. Eiko was saddened by Sayuri's situation at home when she was growing up. Eiko had grown up in a loving family, where her parents spent time with her and her brother. She thought of all the birthday celebrations and family vacations she had enjoyed with her family and decided to pursue the topic.

"Did your parents celebrate your birthday when you were younger?"

Sayuri shook her head. "No. Birthdays were not celebrated. They were not even mentioned."

"Did you ever go on a family trip together?"

Again, Sayuri shook her head. "No. We had a compact car, with only four seats, but we had six people in our family, so travel by car was out of the question. They even thought that six train tickets cost too much, so that was ruled out as well. My parents went on trips, but we were left behind. Occasionally Mother would ask the neighbor lady to check on us while they were gone. We did fairly well until a big storm came or one of us got sick. But even then, we learned how to survive."

Eiko remembered how her family always found someone to watch their cat while they were on vacation. It must have been so difficult for Sayuri and her siblings to be left on their own. Disturbed by what she had already heard, she braced herself for the rest of Sayuri's story.

"My boyfriend and I were best friends," Sayuri said. "We trusted each other and had no secrets between us. We began kissing each other goodbye when we parted company in the afternoon. I always had to be home in time to make dinner for my siblings, especially when my parents went out." She sighed. "I missed him so much in the evenings. He said he missed me, too. He would worry about us being alone.

"Then it happened. My parents were away on one of their trips when a typhoon suddenly turned from its projected path and headed toward our small town. I gathered flashlights, water bottles, snacks, and blankets, and I told my siblings to make sure their bedroom windows were shuttered before meeting me in the living room. We were all together when the doorbell rang. I told them to stay put while I went to see who was outside in the rain. I opened the door and was shocked to see my boyfriend standing there, in his raincoat. He said he was worried about us and decided to come over and spend the evening with us rather than stay at his friend's house. He had even arranged for his friend to pick him up the next day and take him home."

At that moment, an elderly man in the coffee shop started choking and gasping for air. Sayuri and Eiko looked in his direction, as did everyone else. A young man, obviously his caregiver, tried to help the man in his distress, but he didn't seem to be making any progress.

As the manager called for an ambulance, a lady at a nearby table identified herself as a nurse and offered her assistance. She seemed to know what she was doing, and the man was beginning to breathe normally again by the time the ambulance arrived. With a tragedy averted, it wasn't long before the place got quiet once again.

Sayuri looked at Eiko. "I think we should call it a day, don't you? I am too worried about that man to finish my own story. I will have another opportunity some other time. What do you think?"

"You are probably right," Eiko agreed, though reluctantly. She had enjoyed spending time with someone close to her own age and hated to see their time together end. Yet they did have work the next day, and she knew it was probably best to head home. The young women paid for their meals and walked out into the cool evening air, as they headed for the entrance to the train station.

On the ride home and during the walk to her apartment, Eiko couldn't forget the conversation they'd had at the coffee shop. Sayuri's story reminded Eiko of a twenty-four year-old pop star in Japan, whose suicide was recently in the news. After experiencing a loveless childhood, the star chose to end his life instead of seeking help. Although similar in their struggles, it was obvious to Eiko that Sayuri was now happy and peaceful. *I wonder what happened that made a difference. Maybe her parents changed for the better, or maybe her boyfriend helped her through her troubles. Sayuri said her story had a happy ending. I wonder what it could be.*

As she unlocked her apartment door and stepped inside, Eiko wondered when she would be able to visit with Sayuri again. The closer it got to the end of the year, the busier they would be at work. Eiko didn't want to think about the extra hours that would be required at the company over the next three months, so she climbed into bed and let herself drift off to sleep.

The next morning, as Eiko exited the train station to begin her short walk to work, she saw Satoh at the intersection. Hurrying to catch up with him, she called, "Satoh kun! How are you? I have not seen you since the wake."

As Satoh turned to greet her, she noticed how sickly he looked. "Are you feeling well this morning?" she asked.

"Not exactly." Satoh's voice sounded nearly as weak as his face appeared. "I, uh... I got home late from a party last night. This morning it was hard to wake up and put my suit on. I feel as though I forgot something important." He shook his head as if to clear it. "What are you up to these days? Still looking for churches in Tokyo?"

Eiko chuckled as they fell into step together. "No, silly! The church where the wake was held is the only church I have ever been in, and I am not planning on looking for any others if I can help it."

"Actually, Eiko chan, I think church sort of fits you."

Eiko arched her eyebrows in surprise. "What do you mean? Why would you say that?"

He shrugged. "I do not know exactly. But... you just have the kind of personality for church, I suppose. You know, quiet and thoughtful."

"Is that a compliment or a dig?"

"It is just a statement of fact. That is all."

"Well, you are entitled to your opinion."

He paused for a moment, then brightened. "Hey, Eiko, I know a good place to eat a few blocks from here. Do you like ramen? They have several varieties that are all very tasty. That is where I am going for lunch. Would you like to join me?"

As they stepped inside their work building, Eiko remembered that she hadn't made her lunch that morning and didn't have any special plans. "Okay. Where do you want me to meet you?"

"In the first-floor lobby at noon." With that, he turned and headed to the stairwell to climb to the sixth floor.

Eiko waited patiently for the next elevator, preferring the convenience of a lift to the effort of climbing stairs. Once seated at her workplace, she settled in and was busy working when the morning starting bell rang. She was already looking forward to eating ramen for lunch and finding out why this spot was Satoh's favorite.

Sure enough, when Eiko entered the lobby at noon, Satoh was waiting for her, with a twinkle in his eye. "You really should take the stairs, you know. It is quicker than waiting in line for the elevator—and it is good for you."

Eiko smiled, ignoring his comments about the stairs. "It sure looks like you are feeling better. What happened?"

"All I needed was three cups of company coffee—a knife could stand up in that!" He chuckled. "It woke me up and gave me energy for the day."

Eiko accompanied Satoh down the street and around the corner. As they entered the alley, she noticed it was lined with small restaurants. They were greeted warmly when they entered the ramen shop.

"Come in, come in," the workers called out, as Satoh and Eiko were seated at a table for two near the door. It appeared that the restaurant could hold only about twenty customers at a time.

A man's voice from the kitchen snagged their attention. "Satoh kun, so happy to see you today. It has been awhile. Where did you find such a lovely lady?"

Eiko blushed as she saw the older man who had given her the compliment. He had a headband across his forehead, advertising the ramen shop. She nodded silently, as Satoh returned the man's greeting, ignoring his comment about Eiko.

In addition to the older man in the kitchen, Eiko saw two women in white aprons, working beside him. The only other employees were the two young ladies making their way among the customers, taking and delivering food orders.

As one of those workers came their way, Satoh explained to Eiko that he had gone to school with her.

"Would you like your regular ramen today, Satoh kun?" she asked, a smile gracing her lips.

Satoh nodded. "Yes, please."

She turned to Eiko. "And what would you like?"

"I'll have the mountain vegetables ramen, please."

The waitress called out the order to the kitchen staff, then moved on to another table.

As Eiko turned her attention back to Satoh, she noticed he was gazing at her pearl earrings. Before she could ask why, he gave her the explanation.

"Your earrings remind me of a similar pair my grandmother had. They were her favorites. But she passed away ten years ago."

Eiko smiled as she reached up and touched one of them. "Actually, these belonged to my grandmother. My mom passed them to me after Grandmother's funeral two years ago. What a coincidence!"

Satoh nodded. "They look really nice on you."

Eiko blushed and looked down at the table, just as the waitress placed two bowls of steaming ramen in front of them. In moments they were slurping the noodles, one delicious bite at a time.

Satoh was the first to speak. "I think this is the best ramen in Tokyo. I love it! What do you think?

"It is very tasty." She nodded. "And surely the best ramen in Tokyo ... although I think Hokkaido ramen is the best."

Satoh smiled in response as they continued eating. When they were finished, he paid the bill for both of them, though Eiko had offered to pay for her own.

Feeling full and content, they walked down the street and around the corner until they reached their office building. A delivery truck was parked up on part of the sidewalk, bringing goods to the corner convenience store.

Satoh stopped. "That delivery truck just reminded me that I need to stop and buy some batteries for my earphones, so I can listen to music on the train ride home. I will see you back at the office." He bowed slightly to her and disappeared.

Eiko returned to work with a smile on her face. Her time with Satoh had gone well, and she enjoyed herself. She wondered if she would have the pleasure of his company again but pushed the thought to the back of her mind as she began her afternoon work responsibilities.

Later that evening, at home in her cozy apartment, Eiko watched a TV drama while she ate supper. She loved the way she and her mom had decorated the compact living-dining area. A small black sofa sat next to a red reading chair, with a white floor lamp in between. A white frame, with the *kanji*, or character, meaning "success" written in black and mounted inside the frame, hung above the sofa.

The low coffee table was black with red accents. On it sat a black vase with white silk sweet peas and red roses. Eiko had white dishes with red accessories in her kitchen. Red, white, and black had been her favorite colors since high school.

Watching TV dramas was something else that had been one of Eiko's favorites for the last few years. The one she watched that evening involved a family that had many misfortunes in life but always seemed to survive each crisis... until the next one happened. It reminded Eiko of friends she knew. Sometimes it seemed that bad luck plagued certain individuals or families. She had often wondered why but had never come up with a plausible answer.

In tonight's drama, the grandfather character's Buddhist funeral was taking place. Eiko listened as the different characters at the event talked about the grandfather's life.

"He was a kind fellow, but he sure drank a lot," one neighbor commented. "I was there; I know. I picked him up too many times when he fell down."

"Too bad he did not know his grandchildren very well, since they lived far away," an old company friend lamented. "He would have enjoyed teaching them how to fold difficult *origami* animals."

"He was a man of few words," his son-in-law said. "But he loved to paint pictures of nature scenes. He put his best one on the family Buddhist altar as a present to his ancestors."

Eiko watched as loved ones bowed their heads before a photo of the deceased grandfather, taken a few years earlier before he learned he had a terminal illness. After everyone who wanted to say something had an opportunity to speak, the mourners gathered around his simple, open wood casket. Some dropped money in for his journey to the next life. Others placed flower petals around his body. Then the lid was put on, and those who wanted to took a turn hammering in a nail to secure the lid before it was transported to the crematorium. The TV drama ended with scenes for next week's show at the crematorium, where the family would wait for the cremation process to be finished.

Her experience at Mrs. Itoh's wake popped into her mind. None of those things took place at the church. Instead, there were songs and praises to the Lord for Mrs. Itoh's beautiful spirit and generous ways while she was alive. They seemed to know where she was going, too—a place they called heaven. They didn't look worried for her. *Why is that?* Eiko wondered to herself.

As the show ended, Eiko remembered the gift she had received at Mrs. Itoh's wake. She went into her bedroom, opened the drawer, and took it out. Carefully unwrapping it, she discovered the words "New Testament" written on the cover in Japanese. *This must be their holy book. Maybe if I read a little before I go to bed every night, I will learn the secret of the peaceful people at the Christian church.*

Eiko thumbed through the New Testament until a sentence grabbed her attention. "Seek and you will find." The words made her heart beat faster. Didn't that describe her own situation? Hadn't she just voiced her desire to find out about the God the Christians believed in? Eiko continued reading for a few more minutes and then carefully put the New Testament back in her drawer, deciding to watch another TV show before going to sleep.

CHAPTER THREE

Eiko jerked awake with her heart pounding. As she adjusted her eyes in the darkness, she tried to remember her nightmare. The details escaped her, but the fear remained. She decided it must have been the scary movie she watched before bed; it wasn't the first time this had happened. Eiko promised herself she would stay away from horror movies of any kind.

She got dressed in her work uniform, glad that it was easy to look nice every day without worrying about what to wear. She had two uniforms—a summer one they were allowed to wear until early autumn and a winter one for colder weather. Recently, on the appointed day, everyone at work had to make the switch to winter.

Eiko pulled her straight black hair to one side as she tied a blue scarf around her neck. It looked nice against her white blouse and dark blue skirt and vest. Only one more thing and she would be finished. She needed to choose her earrings. She decided on the Rhodochrosite Cabochons mined in Hokkaido—polished orange-colored gems with a smooth dome shape. Office rules required all earrings to be smaller than the earlobe. Dangling earrings could be worn only on weekends or after work.

Once on the train, Eiko closed her eyes in hopes of getting a little nap, while still staying alert enough to count the stops to make sure she got off at the right place. By the time she had ridden the elevator to her work floor, she saw Sayuri, obviously full of energy, walking toward her.

"Good morning, Eiko," her new friend called out. "I wanted to ask you if we can get together tomorrow evening. I would like to tell you the rest of my story of how I met Mrs. Itoh."

Eiko was pleased at the prospect. "Yes. I would like that, Sayuri. Shall we meet at the same restaurant by the train station?"

"Well, that is okay," Sayuri said. "But I am thinking a quieter place might be better, so we are not interrupted like last time. You are welcome to come to my apartment; it is about a one-hour commute from work."

"My apartment is closer to our office," Eiko offered quickly. "You can come home with me, if you like. We can make *gyouza*, pot stickers, for dinner while we visit."

"That sounds wonderful. Thanks!"

Eiko was glad she had gone grocery shopping over the weekend. She already had all of the ingredients needed to make dinner for Sayuri tomorrow evening.

After Eiko got home from work, she straightened up the apartment and had dinner. Later, she enjoyed a hot soak in the *ofuro*, a unique Japanese bathtub, before going to bed. Eiko decided she was too tired to read the New Testament; it would have to wait until another day.

The next evening, the ladies prepared dinner together at Eiko's apartment. Sayuri diced the cabbage, while Eiko prepared the minced pork with scallions and garlic. After combining the ingredients, the ladies placed a spoonful of the mixture in the middle of each one of the small, circular flour wrappers before folding them over and pinching together the edges with a drop of water to seal them. Eiko checked again on the *miso* soup, which had been seasoned with fermented soybeans, with small tofu squares added in. She also checked the rice cooker before she began cooking the gyouza.

In a short time, everything was ready, and they sat down to eat. After saying, in unison, "*Itadakimasu*," meaning "this feast is humbly received," the ladies began to prepare their plates. Eiko noticed that Sayuri had her eyes closed for a few seconds before opening them and then using her chopsticks to help herself to some gyouza. Before taking their first bite of rice and gyouza, they lifted their red lacquer bowls to their mouths to taste the soup. Eiko thought it was perfect, and Sayuri obviously agreed, as she smiled and nodded, indicating her bowl.

Soon, they were eating from the individual rice bowls of steaming *gohan*, or cooked rice, along with numerous gyouza, dipped in a special sauce. It wasn't long before their appetites were satisfied.

Sayuri laid her chopsticks down on her plate and smiled. "Everything is delicious, Eiko."

Eiko nodded in agreement. "Gyouza are always more delicious when eaten with friends or family."

"So true." Sayuri giggled and popped another gyouza into her mouth.

Pouring each of them a cup of ocha, Eiko said, "You were going to tell me the rest of your story, Sayuri. Is now a good time to begin?"

"Sure. Let me think a moment where I left off." She closed her eyes briefly, then opened them and smiled. "Oh, yes, I remember. It was the night of the storm, and my boyfriend came over to help me calm my younger brother and sisters. Well, that night after the storm ended and the kids were asleep, my boyfriend and I gave in to our weaknesses and became intimate for the first and only time. By morning, we agreed that we had acted foolishly and would not repeat our mistake. Both of us were young and had dreams for the future, which included college. My boyfriend's family constantly put pressure on him to make something of himself, so they would be proud."

"How about your parents?"

She shook her head. "No. They never said anything about my future. I think they were hoping I would stay at home and take care of my siblings so they could follow their own dreams. My personal dream was to study art. Several people encouraged my parents to allow me to pursue it, believing that I had a special gift. I mostly did landscapes in watercolors."

Eiko was surprised. "I would love to see your work sometime."

Sayuri smiled, as her cheeks flushed pink. "I only have a few of my art pieces. My life turned out differently. I did not get to study art at college. I had to put it aside."

"Did your boyfriend go on to college?"

Sayuri nodded. "Yes, he did. He ended up graduating with honors—or so I heard from a mutual friend years later."

Eiko felt badly for her friend. "What happened to you? Why did your plans change?"

"I ... got pregnant, and ... I did not know what to do. My boyfriend had already left for college when I found out. He called me occasionally during his first month there, but the calls lasted only a few minutes. After that, he said he was too busy to contact me. He told me his parents were constantly checking on him."

Sayuri sighed, deep and long. "I did not know what to do. I could not tell my parents, and I did not want to burden my boyfriend because I still really loved him and did not want to be the cause of him failing." She shrugged. "I knew I was on my own. Simply said, I worried about what to do so much that I did not eat properly. I got really sick with a high fever. It was not until my next doctor's appointment that my doctor told me what I had feared—I had lost the baby."

Eiko gasped. "Sayuri, how terrible! I am so sad for you."

Sayuri nodded. "It was a sad time, but please remember, Eiko. I asked you not to be sad for me because there is a happy ending to my story, which I am about to tell you."

"Yes, I remember." Eiko smiled. "You said that the other night. Okay, please tell me the rest of the story. What did you do?"

"I was still grieving the loss of my baby with each passing month—until the baby's due date came and passed. Every baby I saw reminded me of my loss. My heart broke each time, knowing I would never see my baby or hold it in my arms. All I could do was go to the temple and pray to the Japanese god that cares for the souls of babies who have died. Each time I went, I left a gift among the many rows of small idols. I left baby shoes, or a small stuffed animal, or even a knitted baby cap on the idol's head. It made me sad when I went there, but I did not know where else to go or what to do to get rid of my guilt and sadness.

"I stayed home a lot and became more and more depressed about my situation." She paused, and Eiko thought her friend's voice broke slightly when she continued. "I even thought about ending my life. One day at a train station, I thought about how easy it would be to jump off the platform as the train was coming in. Many others have chosen to do the very same thing. But that day, at that train station, I saw an older woman handing out pamphlets. I was drawn to her warm smile, and I somehow forced my hand out to receive one. It was an invitation to phone a helpline when faced with problems too big to handle on your own. The pamphlet had a cross on it, showing that it was a Christian group."

"Did you call that day?"

Sayuri shook her head. "No, not right away. It was several days later when I got the courage to call. It was my first time to ask anyone for help. I really did not know how to do that. But the lady on the phone was so kind. She listened to my story and even cried with me. She told me I was going to be okay, that I was created and loved by Creator God."

Eiko saw her friend blink back tears before she went on. "After several months of talking with her by phone via the helpline, I asked the woman if we could meet. She said she had never been asked that question before. As a helpline counselor, she could not arrange a meeting, according to privacy rules. But she told me that she went to a church around the corner from the station, the one where I received the pamphlet, and that she always wore a cross pin on her dress."

Sayuri took a sip of ocha before continuing. "I started thinking that maybe I could go to that church, find her, and talk with her. I just wanted to see if she was anything like the way I imagined her. I finally got the courage to walk by the church and read the sign that listed their meeting times. I was going to go the next Sunday, but my mother got sick and I had to watch my siblings. Several other things came up, and a whole month of Sundays passed before I could try again."

Eiko was captivated with the young woman's story. "How was it when you finally went? Did you feel awkward entering the church? Were people nice to you? Did you find the kind woman?"

Sayuri smiled. "My heart was beating so fast when I walked in and sat on the back row. I guessed there were about seventy-five people there. Several of them smiled and bowed to me as they walked past to get to their seats. Then a man started talking at the front of the church. He talked about how we are like lost sheep. The true Shepherd is motivated by love to go after the lost sheep, he said, because each one of His sheep is very precious to Him. He desires to keep them all close to Him."

Eiko found herself wishing she could hear someone talk like that. It warmed her heart just to think of it.

"The pastor said that the name of our Shepherd is Jesus Christ. Then he read from Psalm 23, which talks about the Good Shepherd and His care for us. As I listened to the pastor talk, I knew in my heart that he was telling the truth. I wanted to meet this Good Shepherd and experience His love and protection. At the end of the service, the man welcomed anyone to the front who wanted to be introduced to this Shepherd, and I knew he meant me. I was so nervous, but I stepped out, not knowing what would happen next."

Eiko swallowed, scarcely able to speak. "And what did happen, Sayuri?"

"When I made it to the front of the church, I saw the pastor already talking with someone. Suddenly, a lady standing near the pastor motioned for me to come. I took a few steps toward her, and that's when I noticed a cross pin on her dress. I started weeping, as she told me Jesus died on the cross to pay for my wrongdoings because of His love for me. Since Jesus was without sin, she said He had the power to forgive me. She also told me that Jesus rose from the dead on the third day, that He is alive, and that He wants to give me the gift of new life in Him—beginning that very moment and for all eternity. Then the lady with the cross pin took my hand in hers and led me in a prayer to receive Jesus Christ into my heart as Savior and Lord."

Eiko's own heart seemed about to burst with emotions she could scarcely identify. "Did...did your sadness and guilt go away, Sayuri?"

She nodded. "It did, Eiko. Jesus removed the sadness and guilt in my heart, and He replaced it with His peace and joy. I realized I had made so many mistakes, trying to do everything on my own. God wants me to ask Him for wisdom to make right choices and also ask Him for strength and courage to follow through. God always hears us when we call upon Him. He never leaves us. He is closer than a friend."

Silence filled the room for a moment, and then she continued. "For several months, the lady with the cross pin taught me what it means to be a follower of Jesus Christ. One day, she told the church members she had cancer. She suffered greatly during her illness but continued to have a warm smile and gentle spirit to the very end. Eiko, that woman was Noriko Itoh, our boss's wife."

"It is almost an unbelievable story, Sayuri!" Eiko said, as she wiped a few tears from her eyes. "What you have shared is very touching. It seems as if the Christian God was searching for you as a lost sheep before you ever knew you had a Good Shepherd who loves you."

Sayuri's smile warmed Eiko's heart. "That is so true. I do not know what I would have done without Him. He is my Savior and Lord, and He means everything to me. The fact is, Eiko, the Bible says God loves everyone just the same. We are all precious to Him. He does not want anyone to be lost."

Suddenly uncomfortable, Eiko changed the subject. "Does Mr. Itoh go to church, too?"

"No, I do not think so. I never saw him there. After his wife died, he asked me about the details of a Christian wake and funeral, and I tried to help him. I think he asked me because he knew I was close to his wife and had also become a follower of Jesus. About two years ago, his wife asked him to find me a job at his company, as a special favor to her."

Glancing at her watch then, Sayuri exclaimed, "Oh, it is getting late, and I should get home. We can talk more another time. Thanks for letting me share with you."

Eiko smiled. "I have been wanting to thank you for your friendship. I was lonely when I first joined the company. You have been very kind to me."

"I believe God planned our friendship ahead of time, before you came. Remember, He is the Good Shepherd."

"Yes. It sounds like He is," Eiko agreed.

The surety of the thought lingered with Eiko, even after her friend was gone. As she finished cleaning up the dishes, Sayuri's personal story replayed in Eiko's mind. As it did, she found herself wondering if she too could ever experience what Sayuri had.

Eiko awoke to another nihonbare morning—not a cloud in the beautiful blue sky. Dressed for work, she left her apartment a few minutes early so she could stop by to see the Sakamotos on the way.

"Ohayou gozaimasu, Sakamoto san!"

The old man looked up at the sound of her voice, a welcoming smile lighting up his pleasant face. "Ah, Eiko chan, *genki*?" Mr. Sakamoto waved to her with his free hand while using the other to place smoked eel in the corner display.

Responding to Mr. Sakamoto's inquiry about how she was feeling, Eiko answered with an assurance that she was doing fine: "*Hai*, genki *desu!*"

"Are you on your way to work?"

Eiko nodded. "Yes, but I have a few minutes before my train comes. How are you doing? How are your sons and Mrs. Sakamoto?"

"All of us are fine," the kind man assured her. "The wife has gone to Yokohama to visit her sister for a few days, and the boys are helping me with the store and the household duties until she returns." As the customers searched for just the right-sized eel for their dinner, Mr. Sakamoto stepped closer to Eiko. "By the way, how was the wake you went to at the church? Were you surprised?"

Eiko paused a moment before answering. "It was…different than I expected, but okay. And you were right; the church people seemed kind."

Mr. Sakamoto nodded, his salt and pepper hair only slightly disheveled. "Yes. That is the part I remember best, even though I only went a few times."

"Actually, Sakamoto san, I just learned that a friend at work is a member at the church where the wake took place. I got to hear her interesting, personal story. She also told me the Bible story of the Good Shepherd. Did you ever hear that one?"

His face lit up. "I did hear about the Good Shepherd, at a children's party at church. Someone even brought a lamb to the church for us to pet."

"Oh, how cute! Lambs are adorable. I love going to Sheep Hill in Sapporo. The sheep always look like they do not have a care in the world." Noticing the customers eyeing her as an inconvenience, Eiko added quickly, "Unlike me, I am afraid. If I do not leave now, I will miss my train. Talk to you later!"

As she hurried down the street, away from Mr. Sakamoto's shop, she heard him calling out the price of smoked eel to his customers. Eiko picked up her pace and ran the last few steps to make it into the train before the doors shut. Standing, since all the seats were taken, she stared out the window as the train rolled along, thinking about her visit with Sayuri the previous night. Eiko wondered what it would have been like to know Mrs. Itoh. *Sayuri was extremely lucky to run into Mrs. Itoh at the train station that day. Is it possible the gods were behind it?* Eiko remembered Sayuri mentioning that the gods at the temple hadn't helped her, and she just got more and more depressed.

When the train doors slid open, Eiko stepped out quickly before the others behind her pushed her forward. As she walked up the steps to her company's office building, she spotted Satoh, a big grin on his face, as he held the door open for her. She couldn't help but notice how handsome he was.

"How are you this morning?" he asked. "How is your week going?"

She smiled, pushing away her thoughts about Satoh. "Very well," she assured him. "Thank you for asking. I have gotten to know Sayuri better, so my week is going well."

"Why don't we eat lunch together so you can tell me about it?" Satoh suggested. "How about the ramen shop? Meet me here after the lunch chimes ring."

Eiko nodded. "Okay. Sure," she answered, watching Satoh leave to climb the stairs to the sixth floor.

At lunchtime, when the two of them arrived at the ramen shop, the line was out the door. Knowing that ramen doesn't take a long time to eat, they were willing to wait. In less than twenty minutes, they were at the door, waiting for the next two available seats.

"Hai, *douzo*," the waitress said as she invited them to enter and sit down.

Satoh teased Eiko that she better not take too long to make up her mind. "Shall I order for us?" he asked.

"No, thank you. I know what I want—the same ramen I had last time."

In less than five minutes, they were once again happily slurping their noodles.

"So tell me, what's been going on?" Satoh asked as he finished his ramen.

Eiko paused from finishing off her own noodles and asked, "Satoh kun, do you believe there is just one God? I mean, have you ever thought about it before? Are you really happy trying to satisfy so many gods to make things work out right in your life?"

Satoh's brief puzzled expression quickly changed to one of surety. "I am proud to be Japanese, if that is what you are asking. We Japanese have always looked for favor and blessing from all the gods available to us. Why wouldn't we? We are free to choose whichever gods we want to worship, and even when and where we want to worship. It is an individual's choice. Don't you feel the same way?"

"Well, yes, I did... until now. Then I heard a coworker talk about her God. She calls Him the One True God, the Creator who made the world and all human beings."

"Not Him!" Satoh shook his head with obvious disdain. "Eiko chan, it is a myth, a total myth spread by foreigners who came to Japan a very long time ago."

Eiko took a deep breath before answering. "No, I do not believe so, Satoh kun. Not the way my friend talks about Him. She communicates with Him and knows Him personally. She said He knows her so well and loves her so much, even though she has made poor choices in her life that were against what He wanted for her."

Satoh's dark eyes were stern. "Some people are not balanced in the head. Your friend must be one of those who will believe anything she is told. I feel sorry for her. She will wake up soon and realize that her god is just like all the others—distant, deaf, and forgetful."

Eiko lifted her eyebrows in surprise. "So that is what you think about the many gods you are trusting in for favor in your life? That they are distant, deaf, and forgetful?"

Looking only slightly sheepish, Satoh admitted, "Well, yes, I guess so. Going to the temple or shrine is like visiting an elderly relative who lives in another prefecture. Because of the distance and lack of time off of work, you can only go once or twice a year. They are old, forgetful, and hard-of-hearing, but you know they still care for you. Going to their place is comforting because you are related to them, even if it has little or no meaning."

"It is not that way with Sayuri's God," Eiko insisted, wishing Satoh had a more positive view of religion. It was obvious he wasn't going to change his mind over lunch, so they got up from the table, paid their bill, and walked back to the office without saying another word on the subject. During her afternoon work hours, Eiko thought often about her conversation with Satoh, but each time it popped up, she pushed it to the back of her mind. When the closing bell finally rang, she was more than ready to go home.

Eiko shivered as she stepped out into the night air and headed for the train station. It was only then that she allowed herself to consider Satoh's comments, yet she knew she couldn't do anything about how he felt regarding religion. She was, in fact, somewhat surprised by how important the topic of religion had become to her.

❧ ❧ ❧

Three busy weeks flew by, with little time or energy to see her friends outside of work. In addition, the flu season was upon them. Many workers were out for a day or two on sick leave, meaning the other employees had to pick up the slack. Eiko had a headache for a few days but not the other symptoms her coworkers talked about. Finally, people came back to work, and everything returned to normal. As a result, Eiko looked forward to the weekend.

Friday night, on her way home, Eiko picked up some take-out food at the curry restaurant. She decided to watch TV in her purple polka-dot pajamas, while eating her favorite curry rice. Halfway through the movie, the phone rang. She wondered who it might be, as she wasn't expecting anyone to call.

"*Moshi moshi*—hello," she said when she answered.

Her mother's desperate voice struck fear in her heart. "Eiko, Papa is sick."

Her heart beat a tattoo against her chest. "Eh? Dad is sick? What happened?"

"He collapsed at work and was taken by ambulance to the hospital. Oh, Eiko, it does not look good. The doctors say they do not know anything yet. He is too quiet and life-less. The only sounds in his room are those made by the machines."

Before Eiko could comment, her mother continued. "I do not want you to worry, Eiko. Papa is going through a hard time, but things will slowly turn around, I am sure. Many people are praying to the gods for his health to return. Eiko, why don't you go to the famous temple in Tokyo and write a prayer for him? He would be happy to know that you have done that for him. That temple is known for prayers being answered for health concerns."

She was already fighting tears as she answered. "Mother, I want to return to Hokkaido. I do not want to stay here in Tokyo while he is in the hospital there. I want to be with him."

Eiko could almost see her mother shaking her head as she answered. "No, Eiko, you must stay at work and do your best. You are still in your first year of employment. It will not be good for you to ask for time off from work. I will let you know when the doctors say your father can have visitors. Then you can come and see him."

Reluctantly, Eiko agreed, but she scarcely slept for worrying about her papa. What really happened to him? Why couldn't her mother understand Eiko's need to be near him? She wanted answers, but it seemed it was up to her to find them.

Sometime in the wee morning hours, she nodded off briefly. She was awakened by a commotion down on the street below her apartment. Giving up on more sleep, she decided to make a light breakfast of toast and coffee, then head out early to the fish market to talk to the Sakamoto family. She needed directions on how to get to the temple where her mother asked her to offer a prayer. The gray clouds, hanging low in the sky, mirrored her own feelings of discouragement after hearing the news that her father had been admitted to the hospital.

When Eiko spotted Mr. Sakamoto, he was welcoming customers and pointing them toward his best deal. Already, the mostly older crowd of women were busy selecting fresh fish for their dinners that evening.

Eiko thought of her own mother not being able to run errands that morning, instead spending the day indoors by her father's side. Her heart ached to be there to help carry the burden.

"*Daijoubu?*" Mr. Sakamoto inquired when he saw the worry on her face. "Is everything all right?"

Eiko shook her head. "No. Today things are not okay. Papa is in the hospital. He is unconscious, and at this moment, the doctors do not know why."

Mr. Sakamoto's face registered his obvious shock. "That is awful! Why don't you go inside and visit with Mrs. Sakamoto until I get free here? I will be up in a little while, after the morning rush is over. The door is open. Go on in."

Eiko walked to the back of the store and headed up the stairway that led to the second-story apartment. Lacking energy, she took her time climbing the stairs. "Sakamoto san, it is Eiko," she called out. "I am coming up the stairs. Sorry to disturb you."

After several seconds of silence, Mrs. Sakamoto appeared at the entryway, wearing an apron over her everyday clothes. "Eiko san, please come in. I was just boiling water for green tea. Would you care for a cup?"

Eiko nodded as she stepped inside. "Yes, thank you. That would be very soothing."

Mrs. Sakamoto frowned. "What is wrong, dear? You look worried."

"I am," Eiko admitted. "I am worried about my papa."

"What is up with your papa?"

"He has been hospitalized in Sapporo, and there is not much hope for him right now."

"That is sad to hear," she said, compassion flooding her voice. "How is your mother doing?"

"She is okay, I guess. She told me not to come home until the doctor recommends it. I guess she is trying to be strong for all of the family."

"Yes, surely she is," Mrs. Sakamoto said as she indicated that Eiko take a seat on the small sofa. Eiko felt comfortable in their modest apartment over the store. Seeing Mrs. Sakamoto so happy in her one-size-fits-all embroidered apron made Eiko smile.

"What exactly happened to your father? Do you know?" Mrs. Sakamoto asked, as she carefully measured out the tea leaves and poured the hot water in the small teapot on the low table nearby. Eiko waited for the gracious woman to put the lid on the pot before she answered.

"All I know is that he collapsed and was taken to the hospital by ambulance. Mother said he has been working a lot of overtime hours at the company because of these hard economic times. She worried that he was not eating regularly and was concerned that he had not been sleeping very well. Mother was sad that Papa would not talk to his employer about the workload. He told her he did not want to be the nail that stuck out to be hammered down."

Mrs. Sakamoto nodded, as she handed Eiko her tea, then brought her own steaming cup and sat down beside her. "It sounds like he needs rest. Maybe this hospitalization is for the best."

Eiko didn't want to agree. She didn't want her papa in the hospital for any reason, even perhaps for a necessary one. But she also didn't want to offend Mrs. Sakamoto by sharing a different view, so she looked away as Mrs. Sakamoto took a sip of her ocha.

CHAPTER FOUR

"**A**re you okay, Eiko san? Is there something I can do?" Eiko could see the genuine concern on Mrs. Sakamoto's expressive, gentle face, and she greatly appreciated it. "Well, actually, there is. My mother wants me to go the famous Tokyo temple, which is known for healing, and write a prayer for my papa. Do you know how to get there by subway?"

The middle-aged woman's face lit up. "What a splendid idea! There have been stories through the years about healing that has occurred there in answer to the prayers offered. I have been there to pray for myself, and although I have not personally received healing, I am still around to keep going back." She chuckled.

At that moment, Mr. Sakamoto walked in, announcing that his son was taking over for a little while so they could all visit. "I need some tea," he announced as he sat down to join them.

While pouring a cup for him, Mrs. Sakamoto told her husband about Eiko's plan to go to the temple in Tokyo to pray for her papa. She also caught him up on what Eiko had already shared about her father's condition.

As Mr. Sakamoto drank his tea, his wife wrote down the directions from the local subway station to the temple, including some helpful landmarks along the way. "It will take about forty-five minutes to get there," she advised, as she handed Eiko the paper with the directions.

Eiko thought that Mr. Sakamoto looked like he wanted to say something, but for some reason he hesitated to give voice to his thoughts.

His wife quickly stepped in. "What is it, my husband? Have I given the wrong directions?"

"No, the directions are fine. I was just remembering years ago when I occasionally attended the Christian church in Hokkaido. I heard the church members say many of their prayers were answered."

Mrs. Sakamoto's eyes widened, and her jaw went slack before she answered. "Husband, are you making this up? I do not remember you ever saying this to me."

He shrugged. "Well, the opportunity never came up all of these years. You knew I went to church several times in Hokkaido when I was young. I strangely remember how much trust they had in their God and how much joy they had on their faces as they waited on their God's answers."

"I think your mind is slipping. You are getting older, you know," Mrs. Sakamoto declared, a hint of teasing in her voice.

"I am just recalling what Eiko chan told us after she went to her employer's wife's wake at the Christian church. She had some questions about what she felt and experienced." Mr. Sakamoto studied her for a moment before continuing. "Eiko chan, after you obey your mother's wishes, you might think about returning to that church and asking them to pray for your father also. That is all I am saying."

Once again, before Eiko could respond, the eldest son, Ichirou, who resembled his father in both looks and mannerisms, quietly entered the room and told Mr. Sakamoto in a low voice that a favorite customer was downstairs asking for him.

Mr. Sakamoto pulled himself to his feet and grunted. "A customer needs me downstairs. Sorry!"

"I need to go, too," Eiko interjected. "I think I will go find the temple this morning."

"See you soon, I hope," Mr. Sakamoto called back over his shoulder as he hurried downstairs after his son.

Mrs. Sakamoto followed up her husband's words by saying, "Yes, come again soon. Please join us for dinner some evening, we hope."

"Thank you," Eiko said as she got up to leave. "That would be nice—sometime."

Mrs. Sakamoto had stepped into the kitchen for a brief moment while Eiko prepared to leave. The woman came back with a small bag, which she put into Eiko's hands.

"Salmon onigiri. Douzo—please—take them for your lunch. There is a picnic area at the temple where you can eat."

Eiko smiled. "I love your salmon onigiri. Thank you for your kindness."

Mrs. Sakamoto returned her smile. "They are fresh— just made them this morning."

"They will be very tasty. *Arigatou*—thank you!"

Eiko slipped them into her shoulder bag, as she made her way to the street, then took a shortcut to the nearest subway station. She was lost in her thoughts as she boarded the subway for the forty-five-minute ride to the temple. With eyes closed, she pictured her papa in his hospital bed and her worried mother sitting by his side.

Eiko took comfort in knowing that her visit to the famous temple and writing out a prayer for her papa would encourage her mother. She would call and let her know as soon as she returned home from her errand.

For as long as Eiko could remember, her parents made a yearly visit to the Hokkaido Shrine in Sapporo during the New Year celebrations. Like most Japanese, they went to seek blessings from the gods for the coming year. Japanese understand that being born in Japan brings with it the cultural responsibility and expectation to carry on traditions that have been passed down for hundreds, if not thousands of years. Eiko thought that neither she nor her brother had truly carried on enough of their parents' traditions, but busy lives simply didn't allow for such luxuries.

When the doors opened at the next stop, Eiko heard an announcement of a regretful delay. The official spoke into the microphone, as he recommended all honorable passengers should consider transferring to another line or be prepared to wait. The gentleman had scarcely finished speaking when passengers began to exit the subway cars. Eiko, on the other hand, was in no particular hurry and decided to wait it out. Only one other passenger in her car did the same—an elderly man sitting near the open door at the other end.

Within minutes, a conductor stepped into the car and looked around.

"Was it a jumper?" the elderly man asked.

The conductor nodded. "Unfortunately."

The old man shook his gray head. "Too many decide to end their lives this way," he muttered, but the conductor had already walked on through to the next car. Speaking now to Eiko only, he continued. "To most, it is just a brief interruption in their day that they soon forget. *Aa, Shu yo*— Oh, Lord!"

Eiko was puzzled by the old man's expression. "Aa, Shu yo" was something she hadn't heard before. Was he calling out someone's name?

She shook her head. *The elderly man is right. Does anyone really care about the reason the train stopped? Do I?* At that moment, Eiko heard a calm, quiet voice speak to her heart. "I care. Remember, Sayuri was helped when she thought of ending her life in front of a train. I sent a kind stranger, who reached out to her with compassion and offered her a lifeline. That lifeline is My only Son, Jesus. The elderly man in the train is one of My followers. Aa, Shu yo is his heart crying out to Me."

"Oh!" Eiko exclaimed aloud as she remembered the details of Sayuri's story. Her heart raced as she looked up and noticed the elderly man staring at her with a concerned look on his face.

"Are you all right, Miss?"

"Yes. Yes, I am fine. Sorry!"

About fifteen minutes later, the warning bell rang, signaling the train was about to leave. The people waiting in the station boarded quickly.

"Sorry for the delay," declared the announcement over the loud speaker. "It could not be helped."

Perhaps it could have, Eiko thought, as she moved over to make room for a young mother and her toddler.

After several stops, the announcer said, "Next stop is the temple."

Eiko focused her attention on making it to the door through the crowded car. It was a relief to finally exit the subway station, climb up the stairs to the street, and walk out into the fresh air. Making her way down the sidewalk, she stopped when she spotted the huge temple grounds looming just ahead.

Oh, these ancient doors! How many centuries have they been there? Looking to one side, Eiko saw a replica of the gigantic straw sandal that loomed over the crowd at the entryway, reminding visitors how big the god was that they were seeking for help.

The direct path to the temple steps was lined with little stores, selling souvenirs and traditional sweets. Eiko wasn't in the mood to shop this morning but made a decision to return another day to see what interesting things were available.

She approached the water purification area and picked up one of the long-handled wooden ladles, which she then used to pour water over her left hand and then her right, as a symbol of being cleansed. Next, Eiko poured a little water into her left hand and with it rinsed her mouth. She let the remaining water flow out to cleanse the ladle.

From there, Eiko visited the incense area. She stood with others, surrounding the large smoldering pot of burning incense sticks. Then she lifted her two hands together, with palms facing her, repeating a forward motion to her face so the incense might cover her. Others standing near her did the same, following the tradition in order to be blessed by the gods.

As Eiko climbed the steps, she found the wooden offering box and threw her money down, past the grate that kept it safe. As the money fell, she placed her hands together and bowed her head in respect. She bowed again and clapped her hands together two times. After a silent prayer, she bowed and stared straight ahead, where she could see the statues and intricate worship area, accessible only to the priests who lived on the temple grounds. Everything seemed dark and eerily cold as she viewed the restricted, lifeless area.

Turning around, Eiko saw the small building where wooden prayer tablets could be purchased. She waited in line until reaching the counter, where she could look through the different prayers to find one that met her mother's expectations. After reading several, she found one that seemed appropriate—a prayer tablet for someone close to death.

She opened her purse and realized she had just enough to purchase it. *That was sure lucky. What if I had not had enough money and returned home disappointed?*

Eiko touched the little wooden tablet with her fingers. She took out a pen and wrote her papa's name and the date on the back. Then she looked at the board where all of the prayers were posted. Her eyes carefully picked the spot where she wanted to tie hers. She noticed several prayers for good grades, a desire for a child or more income, and a wish to be married. But the spot she decided was best was next to several prayers for the sick. *Papa is in good company. If one gets well, maybe they all will.*

Eiko noticed some children running around on the temple grounds, near the place where tour buses let off their passengers. Several benches and vending machines were in the area, as well as restrooms. Her stomach told her it was time to eat, and she was grateful for the onigiri Mrs. Sakamoto had insisted she take for a lunch break.

Eiko washed her hands in the restroom, got a bottled water from the vending machine, and sat down on a bench. She pulled out one of three homemade onigiri and took a large bite. The delicious rice and pieces of salmon were so tasty, she ate a second one. Satisfied, she wrapped the third one up, slipped it back into her bag, and retraced her steps to the subway entrance.

She hoped there wouldn't be any delays on her return trip. She wanted to go home and sleep the afternoon away, waking up in the evening only to call her mother and let her know that she had followed her wishes.

The subway was too crowded to get a seat, so she held on tightly to the handle with her right hand, as she stood and swayed for the forty-five-minute ride. At last, she arrived at her apartment, put her key in the door, stepped inside, and locked the door behind her. Then she went straight to her bedroom and flopped down on the bed. Within a few minutes, the tension of the last two days melted away, and she was fast asleep.

Early the next morning, Eiko's phone jangled on her nightstand, pulling her from a sound sleep. She fumbled for the phone and nearly dropped the receiver before catching it. "Moshi, moshi," she mumbled.

Her mother's voice jarred Eiko to clarity. "Eiko, I am sorry to disturb you, but I think you should come to Sapporo after all. The doctor thinks it might help your father's condition if you were able to visit. I have paid for your plane ticket; you can pick it up at the airport. Your flight leaves at noon. Please do not miss it."

Eiko was stunned. "What are you asking me to do, Mother?" She sat straight up on her bed. "What will I do about work? I cannot just leave without telling someone, and I am not sure who to tell."

"No problem, Eiko. I have contacted your uncle's best friend from college, who is related to your boss. The friend will call his relative, Mr. Itoh, to personally inform him of your situation. Due to Mr. Itoh's wife's recent passing, how could he not be sympathetic?" She paused. "I am sorry, Eiko, but I must get back to your father now. Your brother will pick you up from the airport."

"Mother, how long will I be staying?"

"We will discuss that later, dear. Goodbye."

Eiko heard tears in her mother's voice, which only served to summon her own, though she blinked them back.

"If only Mother had given me some warning," Eiko said aloud, feeling the need to verbalize her feelings. "At first, she said I should not come, and now, suddenly, she changes her mind and demands I get there right away. I wish my mother would think more about my feelings." At the same time, she had to admit that she looked forward to seeing her beloved papa.

Eiko got up, showered, dressed, and grabbed an overnight bag. *It will be chilly in Sapporo,* she reminded herself. Since she already had several coats hanging in her closet at her parents' house, she decided not to pack another one.

With her task completed, Eiko carried her bag to the genkan before going out to let the Sakamoto family know she would be away.

"*Konnichiwa,* Eiko san!" Mr. Sakamoto shouted happily. "How are you this fine fall day?"

"Well, actually, that is why I came to see you," she said, as she drew near and stopped in front of him. "My mother wants me to return to Sapporo today and spend time by my papa's hospital bed. The doctor thinks it might help him wake up from his coma. I leave on a noon flight."

Her friend lifted his eyebrows. "Is everything taken care of? Your plane ticket? A way to get to the airport? Is there anything we can do for you?"

She shook her head. "No. Everything is okay. Mother says my ticket will be at the airline counter. It is easy for me to take the monorail to the airport, and my brother is picking me up in Sapporo. But thank you for your kind offer."

He nodded. "Let us go upstairs and tell the wife. Do you have time for some tea?"

Eiko checked her watch. "Just a few minutes. I need to be on my way soon." Mr. Sakamoto's eldest son was helping a customer, when his father made a motion with his hand that he and Eiko were going upstairs. The young man responded with a nod.

"Eiko chan is here to see us," Mr. Sakamoto called, as he and Eiko walked into the genkan and toward the living room.

Mrs. Sakamoto appeared almost instantly. "Hello, Eiko chan. It is always nice to have you visit. Can you stay for a late lunch today?"

"No, I am sorry. I must go to Sapporo today to visit my papa in the hospital."

The woman's expression changed from pleasantly surprised to concerned. "Oh, dear, I am sorry. Has his condition changed for the worse?"

"I think not, but the doctor hopes my being there might help my papa's condition improve."

"I see." She nodded slowly. "I am sure you being there will be a big help and comfort to him—poor man—and to your mother as well."

She disappeared from the room for a few minutes, while Mr. Sakamoto asked a few questions about the hospital in Sapporo. Then Mrs. Sakamoto reappeared, gently placing an envelope in Eiko's hand. "Please take this, Eiko chan, because it is such an awful time for you."

Eiko guessed the envelope contained money to help her with any unexpected expenses she might have along her way. It was an act that showed the Sakamotos' understanding and good will. "I regret the position this may have put you in," she said softly, "feeling you must help me out in my troubles. But everything is taken care of, really."

Mr. Sakamoto added his opinion. "Eiko chan, you must take it. You never know. It might be useful."

"Yes. We insist," Mrs. Sakamoto chimed in. "Please."

Bending from her waist as she remained seated, Eiko bowed and placed the envelope in her bag, finished her tea, and stood up to leave.

"I will see you when I return," she promised. Then she headed out the door, down the stairs, and through the fish market, clutching her bag and wondering what life would bring her way in the days and months to come.

Still wondering about her future, Eiko arrived at the airport, picked up her ticket, went through the security gate, and boarded the plane with a heavy heart. She dozed off and slept for most of the hour-long flight, then woke up when the flight attendant's voice came on the loud speaker: "All Nippon Airways thanks you for flying with us. We hope your stay in the Sapporo area will be a pleasant one. The local time is one-twenty-five p.m. We hope to have the pleasure of serving you again in the future."

Eiko couldn't imagine her visit in Sapporo being pleasant at all. *How can sitting by my comatose papa, confined to a hospital bed, be anything but painful?* As she passed through the terminal, she glanced up at a large sign that read, "Sapporo welcomes you!" She let out a sigh of relief. Her hometown was special, like no other city, a place of many happy childhood memories. Was it possible she might one day make more good memories here?

Eiko was able to exit right away through the luggage retrieval area, since she had only her small carry-on bag. Many others had traveled the same way, and together they passed through the doors to the main lobby. She looked around for her older brother, Yuitsu, whom she affection-ately called Yu. She spotted him right away, off to the right. With his glasses and pensive look, he appeared to be exactly what he was—a thoughtful, studious young man.

Yu smiled when their eyes met, and he rushed over to her and grabbed her bag. Eiko thought he and her papa looked so much alike. Both loved books and could often be found with their nose in one.

"How was it?" Yu asked.

"The flight? Oh, it was fine. How was your drive to the airport?"

He shrugged as they walked toward the nearest exit, headed for the parking lot. "Fine. No trouble on the expressway."

"And how is... Mother doing?"

"She looks tired. I do not think she is resting well. She spends most of her time at father's bedside."

She nodded. It was what she would expect from her mother. "Has he opened his eyes at all?"

Yu shook his head. "No, not once. It is hard to look at him. He does not look like himself."

She sighed. "Thanks for warning me."

"Try not to think about it. It is better that way." Pointing to a white Nissan two rows away, he said, "The car is over here."

Neither one spoke on the ride from the airport into the city. Eiko was lost in her own thoughts about her parents, and she imagined Yu was as well. As her brother drove, she looked out the window at the familiar scenery. In less than an hour, they pulled into the parking lot of a large hospital.

"Mother asked me to bring you here first. Hope you do not mind."

They picked up guest passes at the information desk and proceeded to the fifth floor, where their father's room was located. Eiko watched the elevator go from the third floor to the fifth, with no floor in between. She knew the number four in Japanese can be read as "death," and that was too foreboding to deal with in a hospital. Eiko appreciated the part of her culture that took people's feelings into consideration. Right now, she wanted to think only about her father getting well and leaving the hospital—no distractions.

"Here he is, room five-oh-three," Yu said as he quietly opened the door.

Upon entering, Eiko saw four patient beds—two on the left and two on the right. The two on the right were empty; an elderly man slept soundly in the first bed on the left. The curtain was pulled around the bed on the far left, obscuring their view. As they made their way toward it, Eiko's mother appeared at the edge of the curtain, with eyes moistened and hands trembling slightly as she reached out to Eiko.

"I am so glad you came, Eiko," her mother whispered. "Thank you, Yuitsu, for picking her up."

"I did not mind at all," Yu said, "but I do need to go back to work now. I will see both of you at home tonight."

Her mother turned to her then and laid a hand on Eiko's arm. "Well, come see your father, Eiko. He has been waiting for you."

Stepping behind the curtain, Eiko laid eyes on her papa. He looked thin and pale, and a vast number of machines monitored his vital signs.

"Hello, Papa," she said, her voice trembling slightly. "It is me, Eiko. I came to see you. I wanted to tell you that I miss your phone calls. I am sorry you are so sick. Get well, Papa. Please?"

The doctor came into the room then and smiled at Eiko. "You must be the daughter who lives in Tokyo." Without waiting for her to answer, he continued. "While you are here, you need to talk to your father. Talk to him like he was listening and very interested in what you are saying. There is a remote possibility this might help." Without any other comments, he checked the tube carrying medicine and nutrition to her father, then turned and walked away.

"He looks too young to be a doctor," Eiko muttered.

"Eiko, please," her mother objected, "he is the top doctor in Hokkaido for this type of injury."

Eiko spent the next three days, taking turns with her mother, at her father's bedside. Late at night, when they finally returned home and Yu was home from work, the three of them would share news with each other about their day. It was tiring, but Eiko was happy to be there, experiencing it with them. Several relatives and friends called the house during that time to check on her father's condition and to tell her "hello" and greet her. Her friends wanted to see her and spend time with her, but she preferred to concentrate on helping her papa get well.

For hours, Eiko talked to her papa about Tokyo, her workplace, her friends—the Sakamoto family, Sayuri, and even Satoh. During those hours, Eiko's mother was able to run errands and take care of pressing needs related to their situation.

On Wednesday morning, Eiko headed to the hospital, knowing that she must return to Tokyo on an evening flight and be back at work tomorrow. Her office had approved three days away, a kind gesture since Eiko had not earned any vacation days yet. But now it was time to go back.

Eiko chose some of her favorite childhood memories to share during her last hours with her papa, like the time her father came to her school sports day and cheered for her, even though she didn't win a prize; the way he explained the different theories of geometry to her, which was the reason she learned to love mathematics. Her voice wavered a bit when she reminded him that he was the one to convince her mother that she should be allowed to move to Tokyo on her own.

Fighting back tears and needing a break, Eiko left the room to get some lunch at the cafeteria. She paid for the lunch special, *oyakodon*—cooked egg and chicken in a sauce over rice, served in a bowl—and a small custard dessert. She also went over to the beverage area and picked up a yogurt drink. As she gazed around the dining room, she noticed an open seat next to two young ladies, who looked about her age. One appeared to be a foreigner and the other Japanese.

"Excuse me," Eiko said in her best English. "I hope you do not mind if I join you."

Welcomed by both of them, she sat down next to the foreign girl with brown wavy hair and freckles.

The young lady smiled as Eiko sat down. She surprised Eiko by greeting her in Japanese. "Konnichiwa. My name is Hope Tanner. Thank you for sitting next to us."

Eiko relaxed and returned the smile. How nice to be greeted in Japanese by a foreigner! Eiko's mind raced to think of an English question she might ask, but Hope was too fast with her next Japanese question.

"My friend, Mari san, and I are visiting a friend of ours who was sick, but she is much better now and should be released to go home soon. How about you? Do you have someone close to you in the hospital?"

The directness of her question surprised Eiko and caused her to hesitate for a moment. "I am afraid so," she finally replied. "It is my papa. He is in a coma, and the doctors do not know the reason why or when he will wake up. I have been visiting him for several days, but I must return to Tokyo tonight."

"I'm sorry to hear that," Hope said, the warmth of her brown eyes stressing her sincerity. "I believe in the power of prayer. May I say a short prayer for him right now, with our eyes open?" When Eiko nodded, Hope began her soft-spoken prayer: "Loving Heavenly Father, we praise You. By the power of Your Son's name, Jesus Christ, please help and heal the beloved father of this family. With thanks, we are praying, amen."

Eiko was surprised to hear such a tender prayer, spoken by a stranger in a public place. She understood that the girl suggested praying with their eyes open because it didn't make what they were doing so apparent. Eiko decided that the young lady, who was about her age, must have had lots of practice to do it so easily. It reminded her of the prayers she heard at the church where Mrs. Itoh's wake was held. She thought about her own prayers that she had said at the temple, as well as the written prayer she had purchased. She didn't know if her prayers were being heard. Did the gods at the temples and shrines know her? Was it out of duty that she prayed? Eiko decided to think about it later, after she said goodbye to the young lady.

"Thank you," Eiko said.

Hope smiled. "By the way, please tell us your name. We will remember to pray for you, too. Maybe we can connect the next time you return to Sapporo to see your father."

Surprised and humbled, Eiko responded, "My name is Eiko. I am sure I will be back to visit my papa. Will you be in Hokkaido for a long time?"

"I will be here for a few more months," Hope answered. "My two-year work assignment is almost over. I am a volunteer at a Christian church, helping out with young people."

Finished with their meals, Hope and her friend got up to leave. "I hope we see each other again," Hope said, her friend echoing her words.

Eiko nodded politely, and the two women left the dining room. An older couple quickly came over to sit in their vacated seats. The couple didn't say anything to Eiko, or to each other. Eiko finished her lunch in silence and returned to her father's room.

CHAPTER FIVE

As Eiko entered her Papa's room, she wondered what else she could talk about. *Maybe I should start by telling him about meeting Hope, or by sharing the questions I have about religion because of my experience at Mrs. Itoh's wake. I bet Papa might be interested in the advice the Sakamotos gave me, or how I left a prayer request at the temple for him.*

With several hours to fill, Eiko was able to share everything she had thought of, including her questions about religion. The last thing she said was, "Papa, I want to know more about the Christian God. The church people and Hope Tanner talk to Him in such a warm, loving way—like He is really listening to them." But by that time, she was too sleepy to go on. She rested her arms and head on the end of her father's bed and drifted off. Even the visitors, who had come to see the man in the next bed behind the curtain, didn't disturb her.

When she awoke, she raised her head and looked at her papa's face. She gasped when she realized his eyes were open. Immediately, Hope's prayer came to mind. Was Hope's God healing her father?

"I love you, Papa," she said, as she grabbed his hand, and tears began to trickle down her face.

Papa's eyes moved slowly in the direction of her voice. When their eyes met, she was certain he was trying to communicate with her, but then his eyes closed once again.

Did I imagine he opened them? She shook her head and spoke aloud. "No. I know it really happened."

Eiko quickly pushed the nurse's call button. When the older woman with short black curls appeared behind the curtain that surrounded Eiko's father's bed, she seemed to focus in on her tears. "Did something happen? Has your father's condition worsened?"

"His eyes opened for just a few seconds," she explained, "and he looked at me."

The nurse's response was immediate. "I will call the doctor," she said, then turned and hurried from the room.

The nurse had no sooner left than Eiko's mother arrived. She stopped short when she noticed Eiko's red eyes and tear-stained face. "What happened?" she asked, as she hurried to her husband's bedside.

Eiko told her about her father opening his eyes, but when her mother didn't respond, Eiko was confused. Didn't she believe her? Perhaps her mother was disappointed that it had been Eiko and not she who had been there when this happened.

Before she could wonder any more, a young doctor stepped into the room and went straight to the patient's side. After examining Eiko's father, he turned to the two women and announced, "I am sorry, but his condition is unchanged." His kind eyes mirrored the compassion Eiko heard in his voice. "This occasionally happens to people in a coma," he explained. "They open their eyes for a brief period, but then they return to their previous condition. I am afraid that is what has happened here. Now, if you will excuse me, I need to get back to doing rounds."

Eiko and her mother exchanged glances but said nothing for several minutes. As they sat, side by side, next to the bed, Etsuko spoke. "Thank you for coming. It means very much to me to see you here at your father's side." She patted Eiko's hand. "But now I know you need to go, so your brother is waiting for you in the parking lot. He has your bag in the trunk, and he will take you to the airport.

It had all happened so quickly that Eiko's trip home was a blur. Now, back in her own Tokyo apartment, Eiko quickly hit the snooze button on her alarm when it went off the next morning. Not at all excited about the day, she waited another thirty minutes before making herself get out of bed. Then she fixed a quick piece of toast and a cup of instant coffee. In ten minutes, she would be heading out the door for work, but right now, she resisted the urge to think of her situation at the office. Instead, she thought about her time in Sapporo. *I wonder if my father would have awakened if I had stayed longer.*

It wasn't until she reached the elevator in her office lobby that she let her mind consider what might be waiting for her at her desk. How much work would she have to make up? Would her coworkers be angry or jealous of her being allowed to miss those days without any vacation time to draw on? As she got off the elevator, she saw Sayuri. They greeted each other with a friendly "ohayou gozaimasu" and a smile.

"You were missed, Eiko," Sayuri said. "It is nice to have you back."

Eiko was encouraged by her friend's words. As they walked together to Eiko's desk, Sayuri told her that the lady whose desk was next to Eiko's had offered to take care of a lot of Eiko's responsibilities while she was gone. Eiko smiled at the news, realizing it was the same woman Eiko had helped before. "How very kind. I will have to thank Akiyama san."

Sayuri placed a small envelope on Eiko's desk, then walked back to her own work space. Eiko was glad Sayuri hadn't asked for any details about her papa. She just wasn't ready to talk about that yet.

The woman who had helped with Eiko's work arrived as the starting bell sounded. Eiko smiled at her and opened her computer, ready to begin work. A conversation and expression of gratitude would have to wait until break time.

The morning flew by, and Eiko hadn't even realized the time until she began to notice her coworkers heading to the break room for coffee and tea. She quickly pulled out a box of cookies from Hokkaido, which she had picked up at the airport on her way home. They were made at a well-known monastery on the island, so she was certain her fellow employees would enjoy them.

When she arrived at the break room, she opened the box of individually wrapped cookies and placed them on the table. *Oohs* and *aahs* immediately broke out at the sight of the popular Hokkaido treat, and Eiko was pleased that she'd had a chance to pick them up to share with the others.

"The first time I had these cookies was when I made a trip to Hokkaido about ten years ago," one woman said. "How nostalgic!"

It is amazing how an unexpected gift brings such delight, Eiko thought.

Then she spotted the coworker who sat at the desk next to hers. She was already heading out the door, back to her work space, so Eiko moved quickly to catch up with her. "Thank you, Akiyama san, for your help during the time I was away," she said, as she drew up next to her. "It really saved me from lots of trouble, but I am sorry you were overworked."

Mrs. Akiyama smiled. "Not at all. You did the same for me when I had to leave work early."

"But you were only gone for half a day," Eiko reminded her. "I was absent for several. You accepted a much heavier burden."

"Think nothing of it." She smiled as she sat down at her desk.

Eiko finished up her morning work just as the noon chimes rang out. She hadn't had time to make an obentou at home before she left, so she decided to go to the noodle shop. A bowl of ramen would taste good.

No sooner had she walked down the street and around the corner than she heard her name being called. "Eiko chan, wait up!"

She turned to see Satoh trying to chase her down.

"Are you headed to our favorite spot?" he asked.

"Yes. In fact, I am."

"May I join you?"

She nodded. "If you like. But I may not be very good company today."

"Why is that?" Satoh frowned. "What could be wrong on this fine autumn day, with a perfect nihonbare that shows off the bluest sky with no clouds in sight?"

"I just got back from seeing my papa in Sapporo. I was absent from work for several days."

His face softened. "Sorry, Eiko chan. I did not know. I have been really busy at work recently, trying to get some reports finished on time. I have not spoken with friends or family for a couple of days. How is your papa?"

"It is a long story. I don't really want to talk about it now."

Satoh nodded. "Okay. Maybe we can talk another time— this weekend maybe? I have to attend my cousin's wedding in Yokohama. My family is expecting me to show up with a date. They always tease me that I come alone to family gatherings. I was wondering if you could help me out by going with me. If you do not feel like it, I will not blame you at all. I was just hoping you would agree to come, since you are the only one I have ever been to church with."

Eiko lifted her eyebrows, as surprised as she was curious. "What? The wedding is at a church and not a hotel wedding chapel?"

"Yes. That is what the invitation says. My cousin is marrying a pastor's daughter. I thought you would be interested. It will be your chance to check out another church and see what it is like. How about it? Will you go with me?"

Eiko didn't really want to be considered Satoh's girlfriend by his family, but her desire to learn more about the Christian God was enough to get her to accept his invitation.

"All right. Yes, I will go with you. What day? On Saturday?"

Satoh smiled as he answered, obviously pleased that she would accompany him. "No. It is on Sunday, in the early afternoon, after the morning church stuff is finished. My relatives have asked us to get there early and attend church too, before the wedding. But if you don't want to, I understand. I can make up an excuse. I would rather not go early myself."

"I think we should," Eiko insisted. "We have only been to a wake. It might be nice to see what goes on in happier times."

Satoh shrugged. "Okay. I will let them know that two will be coming for the church service and for the wedding."

They had moved to the front of the line by now and were soon invited to sit down at a table where another couple had just left.

"Perfect timing," Satoh said with a smile. "I am starved!"

71

"Me, too." Eiko wondered if she had made a mistake by agreeing to attend the church service and the wedding with Satoh, but she kept her question to herself.

Back at her desk after lunch, Eiko still couldn't stop thinking about the upcoming event. The more she thought of it, the more excited she became. She hadn't realized until that moment how much she wanted to go to another event at a church.

Her one regret, however, was not being able to spend time with Sayuri on Sunday afternoon. She thought of the envelope her friend had left on her desk earlier that day. It was an invitation to Sayuri's apartment, one that Eiko would otherwise gladly have accepted. In the note, Sayuri said she had been praying that Heavenly Father would show His loving kindness to Eiko and her family during this difficult time. Sayuri ended the note by saying she was willing to listen anytime Eiko wanted to talk about her father and her trip to Sapporo. *Maybe next weekend we can get together to talk*, Eiko thought, as she focused once again on her work.

Eiko managed to get through her assignments that week and enjoyed relaxing on Saturday. When Sunday rolled around, she found herself both pleased and nervous about the plans she had made with Satoh.

She sighed and took one last look at herself in the mirror by the front door, slipped into her black heels, and walked out into the sunshine. She carried a jacket since it would be breezy near the ocean in Yokohama.

"Satoh kun, ohayou gozaimasu, she called when she first spotted him. "Don't you look nice in your black suit and purple tie!"

Satoh grinned. "It is nice not to have to wear the gray company suit on the weekends." He paused, seeming to size her up in one quick glance. "By the way, you sure look trendy in your green skirt with your brown leather jacket."

Eiko felt her cheeks flush. "Thank you. It is autumn now, so I can wear it."

"Are you sure you are ready to do this today?"

She nodded emphatically, as the train pulled up and stopped in front of them. "Yes, I am. Although I do hope to ask you a few questions about your cousin on the train ride to Yokohama."

"Of course," Satoh said as the doors opened and they stepped inside.

During the hour-and-a-half ride, Eiko learned that Satoh's cousin, Aki, was two years older than Satoh and that he met his bride, Yoko, at a summer church camp when they were in junior high. Aki started going to the same church after that, just to see her, and he soon learned that her father was the pastor there.

As Satoh and Eiko got off the train and began to walk to the church, Satoh said, "This church is easy to find, and it is on a well-traveled road. It is twice as big as the church in Tokyo, where we went for Mrs. Itoh's wake. My cousin has told me all about it."

Eiko nodded, a sense of excitement building inside. She wondered why she had never felt this excited when she was on her way to a temple.

Once inside, they were greeted by smiling men and women, who welcomed them warmly and led them into a large room for the worship service. As the organist played, Satoh and Eiko found seats on the end of a row, about halfway up on the left side. When Satoh spotted his family members in the front rows on the right, he pointed them out to Eiko.

The organist finished playing then, as a man walked up to the mic at the podium. "We welcome you to this special Lord's Day service," he said. "Let us begin with a moment of silent prayer."

Eiko and Satoh looked around and noticed that people had their heads bowed, so they did the same. After a few moments, the man at the podium spoke again. "Let us give the Lord the praise He is due. Would you please stand and sing together hymn number three-four-three?"

After more singing and another prayer, a small youth ensemble got up to give a special presentation. As the group sang, one young man strummed a guitar, and a young lady jangled a tambourine.

The teenagers have such beautiful expressions on their faces, Eiko thought. *As if singing this song is the best thing in the whole world they could be doing.* The words to the song were about Jesus, and the tempo was joyous. Eiko enjoyed it so much that she was disappointed when it ended.

Satoh didn't seem to be paying attention. Eiko noticed him looking at his watch more than once. She gently nudged him in the ribs and silently encouraged him to listen, but by the time he did, the youth ensemble's presentation was over.

The next thing listed on the program, which they had received when they came in, was the pastor's message, titled "What a Friend We Have in Jesus."

That should be interesting, Eiko told herself. *Maybe this will explain how the church people can speak with such warm hearts when they pray to their Christian God.*

Satoh already had his head down in sleep mode, which disappointed Eiko, but she didn't let it dampen her desire to listen and learn.

"Today I would like to talk about Jesus, friend of sinners," the pastor said. "The religious leaders of Jesus' day accused Him of being friends with the wrong people. They did not want to see Him spend time with sinners, people who had done bad things. Their own pride tricked them into believing they always did everything right. But to the people who knew and admitted they were sinners, Jesus brought hope and purpose to their lives. They were thankful to experience His love and forgiveness. The religious leaders would miss out because their hearts were closed to the Truth."

Eiko continued to listen as the preacher talked about how Jesus is the only One who can take away our sins because He Himself never sinned. "God's only Son, Jesus, left the splendor of heaven to come down to earth to be born as a baby in human flesh," he said, "to live among us and to teach us how much Creator God loves all people. Then Jesus died on the Cross to take our punishment and pay the penalty for our sin. God raised Him from the grave after three days. Anyone who admits they are a sinner and trusts in Jesus to save them, becomes a new person from the inside out."

The man paused briefly, giving time for his words to sink in. Then he continued. "When God looks at the people who have trusted in Jesus, He sees only His beloved Son, and not their sin any longer. Trusting in Jesus as Savior and Lord satisfies our longings to be loved unconditionally. It also gives us true purpose for living, which is to worship Him. Jesus promises to always be with us, no matter what we go through in life. He encourages, leads, and guides those He saves, and promises that each one's spirit—or soul—will live forever with Him in heaven when their days on earth are finished. Jesus conquered death so we would know this is true."

The idea of heaven is nice, Eiko thought, as her mind wandered for a few moments. *Papa might like heaven. I know he would like Jesus if he met Him, especially since Jesus is described as a compassionate and loyal Friend.* She thought then how her papa had friends, but not many came to visit him in the hospital because they didn't know what to say or do for him.

She was brought back from her thoughts when the music started again, and a man began to sing "What a Friend We Have in Jesus." Eiko hadn't realized the message had concluded, but now she felt her heart pounding inside her chest. It felt like Someone invisible was tugging at her. Confused, she was glad when the song ended.

The pastor then raised his hands in the air, over the people, as he prayed for God's protection and blessing upon them during the week. The pianist played a brief chorus, and then people started moving around. Eiko thought the time had gone by quickly. She looked at Satoh, who had already found his cousin up front and was giving him a hug.

Eiko didn't know whether to wait for him to invite her over to meet his relatives or whether she should go over that way to remind him she was there. Before she could decide, a young girl came up to her and said she was glad Eiko was there.

Eiko smiled, pleased at the girl's warmth and friendliness. "Thank you. I am Eiko. What is your name?"

"I am Mariko," the girl said, a big smile on her sweet round face. "My daddy is the preacher," she declared with pride.

"Oh, I see. That is nice." Eiko could see why Mariko would be proud of her father. "How long has your daddy been a preacher at this church?"

"All of my life." She giggled. "I am twelve."

Eiko smiled. "What school do you go to?"

"It is just down the street. But I start junior high school in April, and I will have to ride the train."

Their conversation was interrupted when an older woman appeared in a nearby doorway and called out, "Please excuse yourself, Mariko, and come help, please."

Mariko quickly complied and scurried out the door on a mission. Eiko was a bit surprised to see men moving furniture and setting up tables right around her, in the same space everyone had sat during the church service.

Satoh and his relatives were no longer in the room, and Eiko imagined they were checking to be sure all the wedding details were complete. She looked around, trying to decide what to do, and then she spotted Mariko, coming toward her.

"Would you like to buy an obentou for 500 yen?" she asked. "There are two kinds—fish or beef. Usually the church ladies prepare lunch for everyone, but there is a wedding this afternoon, and the ladies have made lots of food for the party afterward. Today it was easier to sell obentou."

Eiko was feeling hungry, and Mariko was being especially helpful. "Sure." She nodded. "Thank you. I will take the fish obentou, please."

She took out her coin purse and handed the exact amount to Mariko.

"You can sit right here," the girl said, pointing to the nearest table, where people were already sitting down and starting to eat.

"Mariko chan," Eiko said, "I should buy one more obentou. Someone came with me to church today."

"I have one beef obentou left. Is that okay?"

"Sure. Arigatou. Here is 500 more yen. You have been very helpful."

"Don't mention it at all," Mariko said with a smile, as she turned to leave.

Eiko sat down and placed Satoh's obentou on the table next to hers. She opened the lid to her own obentou and saw that her meal consisted of fish, rice, glazed sweet potato pieces, and pickles. *Looks good*, she thought, as she picked up her chopsticks and began to eat. After she had eaten a few bites, a man brought around a tray of ocha.

"Would you care for some tea?" he asked with a slight bow.

"Yes, please. Thank you for your kindness." The man had no sooner handed her some tea and stepped away than Satoh appeared. "Please forgive me, Eiko. It could not be helped. My relatives sent me on an errand, which I felt I had to do, but I am here now."

"Oh, I see." She nodded. "I wondered where you had gone. Here is an obentou for you. They only had beef left. Sorry."

"That is fine because I am so hungry. How is yours?"

"Very tasty. I think I have seen the same obentou shop in Tokyo near my apartment. I should go there sometime and see what else they sell."

Eiko was curious about the errand Satoh was asked to do at the last minute, but she didn't want to press him to share the details. *If we are truly friends, he will tell me later.*

When lunch was over, the men quickly set up the room for the wedding. The chairs were put in rows, the tables folded and hidden away. The women decorated the room with flowers and rolled out the white cloth down the middle aisle for the bride to walk on. Beautiful lace tablecloths were spread over the few tables that remained—one in the entryway, two in the back of the room, and one up front. With everyone's help, the room was beautifully transformed in less than thirty minutes.

The bride and groom, along with some members of their family, were each in separate rooms, getting dressed for the ceremony. Soft music played throughout the church, as the aroma of sweet-smelling flowers filled the air. The men had put their suit jackets back on, and the women had taken their aprons off and were gathering the children, who had been playing outside.

It wasn't long before the guests began to arrive. Eiko looked at the people around her—some elderly, others middle-aged, with a nice group of young people also present. Eiko signed the guest book and presented her cash envelope. A few moments later, she was escorted into the large room and chose to be seated on the groom's side. She looked for Satoh and saw that he was still standing in the entryway, talking with someone. Eiko laid her bag down on the chair next to her to save him a seat.

A few more people came in, with Satoh following behind. When he spotted Eiko, he flashed her a boyish grin and came and sat down beside her.

"Thanks for saving me a seat. I did not know if you would."

Eiko grinned as she teased him. "We did come together, remember?"

Satoh grinned, his dark eyes hinting at mischief. "We did? Oh, yes, that is right. I remember now. I hope we can go back to Tokyo together, too, when this is all over."

She laughed. "Yes, of course. How long will we be here after the ceremony is over? Are we staying for the celebration party after this?"

Satoh nodded. "I think you will like it. My cousin said the church has really done a lot for their wedding. The church members' labor of love on their behalf has been more than his fiancée and he expected, or even hoped for."

Eiko looked around the sanctuary again. The flowers were arranged with skill and grace, as were the other decorations. The church had been cleaned and polished, highlighting its unique charm, even though it was an older building. The program was printed on quality paper and had a photo of the couple on the back page, along with a note thanking everyone for their attendance and support of their wedding.

These people know how to do a wedding so beautifully, Eiko thought. *I could be happy with a church wedding myself.*

Before she could take that thought to another level, the pastor and the groom came out of a side door, as the pianist began playing, slowly and reverently, Johann Sebastian Bach's "Jesu, Joy of Man's Desiring."

Everyone turned their eyes to the back of the church, as the pianist continued to play. Twelve-year-old Mariko appeared in an ankle-length red dress, with a matching red bow in her black hair. She held two long-stemmed red roses in her white-laced, to-the-wrist gloves. She smiled, as she took her time walking down the short aisle. Behind her followed her older sister, the bride, dressed in a beautiful red, white, and gold kimono. Her hair was swept up off her neck and held in place with a lovely golden-butterfly hair ornament. She held in her hands a small white bouquet of lily-of-the-valley flowers.

Eiko thought that Satoh's cousin, Aki, had chosen a beautiful bride. As the lovely young woman walked down the aisle toward the groom, her face shown with a special serenity and grace. Eiko couldn't help but notice how Aki couldn't take his eyes off of her.

Once Yoko reached the front of the church, Aki stood by his bride while the pastor read 1 Corinthians 13, "the love chapter," as he called it, from the Bible. A special song followed. Eiko thought the words were rich in meaning, as they told how deeply Almighty God loves us. He purposed that we would be born, given physical life. He also desires to make us spiritually alive, but He waits upon us to make the decision to believe in Him as Savior and Lord, not just as Creator. The young man sang with a smooth voice and compassionate eyes, as the words stirred Eiko's heart.

Eiko looked at Satoh, who seemed to be listening intently. When it was over, the pastor spoke concerning their marriage vows.

"Promises need to be made from the heart willingly but with much soul-searching beforehand. God is a faithful God who keeps His promises, and He will give us grace and strength to keep the promises we make to our mate. Marriage is not always easy. Many challenges will occur, but God's Word says that if we believe in Him and seek His help, we can know a love for our mate that deepens and endures through the years."

He turned slightly toward the groom. "Aki san, please repeat after me as you place the ring on Yoko's ring finger."

The pastor paused, as Satoh's cousin, his hands appearing to shake only slightly, placed the ring on Yoko's finger.

The pastor began again, with Aki repeating after him. "This ring ... symbolizes my deep love ... for you as my wife .... I promise to love you and take care of you ... in good times and bad ... thinking of you first before my own needs."

It was Yoko's turn. "Yoko san," the pastor said, "please repeat after me. This ring ... symbolizes my deep love ... for you as my husband .... I promise to love you and take care of you ... in good times and bad ... supporting you in every way as you guide our family in the ways of God ...."

When the reciting of vows was complete, the pastor looked to both of them. "Let me pray for you. God, thank You for the gift of Your love and salvation that Yoko and Aki each received when they were younger. And now, with your help, oh, God, let their love for each other, and for You, blossom and mature. Bless their lives together for Your glory. I ask in Jesus' name, the name above every name in heaven and in earth. Amen."

Holding hands as friends, the beaming bride and groom looked ready to begin their lives as a married couple, devoted to Jesus Christ. Spontaneous applause broke out as Aki and Yoko walked back down the aisle, side-by-side and hand-in-hand, with music filling the room. A few people wiped happy tears from their eyes, as others mirrored the radiant smiles of the bride and groom.

The pastor then invited everyone to stay for a light meal, followed by the cutting of the beautifully decorated wedding cake.

Satoh and Eiko accepted, but once they had eaten the delicious food, including a piece of cake, which proved to be as delicious as it looked, they excused themselves from the party. Leaving the ongoing celebration behind, they hurried to the train station and boarded the rapid express train back to Tokyo.

The train was crowded, so Satoh and Eiko were forced to share a small space by the door. They stood silently, looking out the window at the passing scenery. After the third stop, some seats became available, so they sat down next to each other.

"Did you have a good time?" Satoh asked.

She nodded. "It was memorable. I am glad I decided to go."

"Are you tired? I sure am," Satoh confessed.

"It was a long day, what with going to the morning church service, then the wedding and party afterward. I am tired but definitely not hungry." Eiko smiled. "That was quite a feast after the wedding, even though they called it a light meal. I heard the ladies wanted to make the food as a gift to the newly married couple."

"Amazing, since wedding businesses charge for everything."

"That is true," Eiko agreed. "Your cousin's wedding was very beautiful, yet simple."

"I don't know about weddings," Satoh mused, "if they are needed or not. I think they are okay for some people. All I want is to do the legal paperwork at the district office, writing down that there are two cohabiting at the same address."

Eiko was surprised by his comment, but before she could respond, the train reached their stop. "See you tomorrow," she said, as she ran across the platform to the waiting local train. As soon as she was onboard and near a window, she glanced out at Satoh.

"Tomorrow," Satoh mouthed as he waved, then turned and headed for a stairway that led to another train line inside the big station.

CHAPTER SIX

A t home in bed, Eiko's mind was busy, as she tossed and turned in her sleep. The next morning, she dragged herself out the door for work and allowed herself to doze on the train ride. She scarcely remembered getting from the train to her workplace.

"Eiko!" Sayuri called out, coming up to stand beside her at the entrance to their office.

Eiko blinked and stifled a yawn. "Ohayou gozaimasu, Sayuri," she managed.

"How was your weekend?"

"Busy." Eiko shook her head, as they stepped through the main door into the building. "Sorry I could not meet up with you. Would you like to go out after work one day this week?"

Sayuri nodded. "Yes, I would like that. Let us do it on Friday. Is that okay? Then we won't have to worry about work the next day."

"Yes, Friday is good," Eiko said as they waited for the elevator.

Once at her desk, Eiko immediately got busy doing her tasks for the day, even skipping lunch to stay ahead on her reports. At five o'clock, she straightened up her desk, gathered her things, and headed to the train station at a quick pace, hoping to catch an earlier train for home. She just made it, then dozed off to the gentle rhythm of the train on the tracks, not waking up until the person next to her stood to get off.

Alarmed, she peered out the window. *Oh, no! I have missed my stop.* She gathered her things and hurried out the train door before it closed.

While walking up and over the train tracks to the other platform to catch a train going back in the other direction, she noticed a young foreign lady in the crowd of people. As the woman got closer, Eiko couldn't believe her eyes.

"Excuse me, but I think I met you recently in Hokkaido," Eiko said when the young woman stopped beside her, put her suitcase down on the platform, then smiled warmly.

"I was thinking the same thing. We met at the hospital, didn't we? Your name is Eiko san, and I prayed for your father, who was in a coma."

Eiko was amazed at the woman's remembrance of details, particularly the prayer for her father. "That is right. And you are Hope Tanner, in Hokkaido for two years, working with young people at a church. How unusual to meet you in Tokyo at this train station! Are you here for a visit?"

"I was just here for a meeting," she replied. "I am headed to the airport now." Before Eiko could respond, Hope asked, "How is your father doing?"

As the train pulled into the station and they prepared to board, Eiko replied, "He is about the same." She wanted so much to tell Hope about how papa's eyes had fixed on hers, but she had to hurry or risk missing her train.

They bid each other farewell, pausing only long enough for Hope to hand Eiko a small name card, which Eiko tucked into her purse. She turned to wave goodbye just before boarding and saw Hope return the wave, as she called out, "Goodbye. Take care!"

Settling into one of the few vacant seats, Eiko was still deep in thought about meeting Hope at the station. What if she hadn't fallen asleep but had instead gotten off at her normal stop? Or what if she had slept longer and traveled farther? Was it really all just a coincidence?

Walking past the fish market on her way home, she heard Mr. Sakamoto call out to her. "Eiko san! How are you? We haven't seen you in a few days. Is everything okay?"

Eiko stopped to greet her friend. "I am okay. Just a busy weekend. How are you? And your family?"

"The same as always." He grinned. "Surrounded by fish."

Eiko smiled and scanned the market, taking in the varied supply of fish for sale. "Yes, I can see that."

"How is your papa, Eiko? My wife and I are worried about him and your family."

"You are very kind, Sakamoto san." She swallowed an unexpected lump in her throat. "Actually, I have not heard anything from my mother since I returned to Tokyo. I should call and check."

"I am sure you would have heard if something had changed in your father's condition. Do not worry."

She nodded. "Yes. I guess you are right."

Mr. Sakamoto paused before speaking again. "Eiko chan, may I ask you for a favor to please my wife?"

Eiko nodded. "Of course. What is it?"

"Will you come by and eat dinner with us next week?"

"Arigatou gozaimasu" she answered with a thankful heart. "I would love to."

Mr. Sakamoto's face mirrored his pleasure. "When is the best time for you?"

"I have Wednesday evening free. Will that work for you and Mrs. Sakamoto? If so, what time should I come?"

"Wednesday is perfect. How about seven-thirty, after I close up the market?"

Eiko nodded again. "Yes. Shall I bring something?"

"No. Only yourself," Mr. Sakamoto replied.

Eiko grinned and waved, as she turned to head for home. A few minutes more and she would be in her own comfortable surroundings, relaxing at last after a busy weekend.

Eiko put the key in her door and stepped inside her small genkan. Leaving her shoes by the door, she headed to the kitchen to make some dinner. Heating up leftover curry rice was quick and easy.

After eating, Eiko sat down at the table and opened her bag, looking for the card Hope Tanner had handed her. She pulled it out and discovered a cross printed on it, along with the words, "...But I call you friends, because I have made known to you everything I heard from my Father." Underneath the words was a reference that read, "John 15:15, (NCV)."

The pastor said in his message on Sunday that Jesus is a Friend of sinners, she recalled. She also remembered the title of the song that the soloist sang: "What a Friend We Have in Jesus."

She frowned. *But this seems to be saying something different. It says He calls us friends, but are we not sinners?*

Eiko thought about that as she cleaned up the kitchen. *Why would Jesus want to be my friend? What does that do for Him? How can Christians believe that their God wants a close relationship with them?*

She still pondered those questions, as she climbed into bed that night. Her thoughts quickly gave way to her weariness, and soon she was fast asleep.

Eiko woke up refreshed the next morning, actually looking forward to her office work, as she believed it would keep her from thinking too hard about other things.

❧ ❧ ❧

Friday had come at last, and it was time to meet Sayuri at the restaurant. Eiko got there ahead of her friend, who had to run an errand first.

Eiko spotted a small green public phone just outside the restaurant door, so she decided to call her mother while she waited. She took out her phone card and dialed. Two rings, three rings…Eiko was about to hang up when she heard her mother's voice.

"Mother, it is Eiko. How is everything going? Any changes in Papa's condition?"

She could almost see her mother shake her head before answering. "Eiko, your papa is still the same. He has not awakened yet. And now, the doctors have said he is at risk of getting pneumonia."

Eiko's heart twisted in pain. "I am so sorry, Mother. That makes me so very sad. How are you doing? Are you holding up? How is Yu?"

Etsuko answered the last question first. "Your brother never comes around the hospital. It is too difficult for him to see your papa like that."

"Oh." Eiko truly wished her brother would spend more time with their parents right now, but she could also understand how difficult it must be for Yu.

Her mother sighed, then went on. "As for me, I am okay, Eiko. Just very tired. I stay with your father every day from morning until night. Then I go home and try to get some sleep. Once or twice your uncle has come to relieve me, so I can run some errands that need to be done."

"Mother, do you need me to come and stay?"

"No, I do not want to burden you. You are young and need to be a good employee so you can establish yourself.

You already came once. I appreciated you doing that for us, and I know your father would appreciate it too. As for any change in your father's condition, it is mostly up to him now, when he decides—*if* he decides—to wake up. People at work have visited the local Buddhist temples and Shinto shrines to purchase prayers for him. Soon the gods will hear and respond."

Eiko didn't know how to answer, as her mother's words caused her to question why their religious traditions made them feel empty and without hope. Did their traditional gods even know who was asking, who was needing help, or how lonely they felt?

Eiko talked a few minutes longer before saying goodbye. She had just clicked off when Sayuri showed up, dissipating Eiko's lonely feeling.

"Hi, Sayuri," she said, smiling for the first time since before she called her mother. "Are you hungry?"

Sayuri nodded. "Yes. I am hungry—ravenous! Let us go in and get a booth so we can order."

As soon as they were seated, the two young women perused the menu, both deciding on the *tonkatsu* dinner special, which consisted of fried pork, a serving of rice, chopped fresh cabbage with house dressing, pickles, and miso soup. Afterward, a tiny dish with sorbet would be brought out for dessert.

For the first few minutes after receiving their food, they spoke little, savoring each bite. About halfway through the meal, Sayuri exclaimed, "This is delicious! I should order this more often."

Eiko swallowed a bite of rice before answering. "I agree. It makes a nice meal, especially to enjoy with friends. By the way, this weekend I went to a wedding at a Christian church. Satoh's cousin Aki got married."

Sayuri appeared genuinely pleased. "That is wonderful! How did it go? Did you enjoy it?"

Eiko nodded. "Yes. Actually, I did enjoy it—very much. We were there for the church service and stayed for the wedding in the afternoon. During the in-between time, they sold obentou to those who wanted to stay for lunch."

"I see." Sayuri took a sip of tea. "You had a long day then. Did Satoh stay the whole time? Was he at the church service with you?"

"Yes. He was there—except for about thirty minutes right after the service finished. He said he was with his relatives, doing something. Actually, I did not even get to meet his relatives personally because he did not introduce me to them. I guess he was just nervous about being in church."

"You are probably right."

Eiko hesitated before speaking again. "I...I want to ask you something, if...if it is okay."

Sayuri shrugged. "Sure. Go ahead. What is on your mind?"

Eiko took a deep breath and plunged forward. "The preacher said in his message that Jesus is a Friend of sinners, and then a soloist sang, 'What a Friend We Have in Jesus.' You are a Christian, Sayuri. I want to know if this is true. Why would Jesus want to be friends with bad people?"

Eiko noticed Sayuri hesitate for a moment before answering. She wondered if her friend might be praying silently to the Christian God.

"Eiko," Sayuri said then, "that is a good question. The Bible tells us that God is a very loving God. He made the world, with everything in it, for us to enjoy. Everything God made was good. But when God made the first people, Adam and Eve, the Bible says it was *very* good. He loved humans from the beginning. One very important part of His love is giving us free will to make our own choices. Creator God wanted people to *choose* to love Him, rather than be *forced* to love Him. Adam and Eve hurt God with their choices. God is holy and just, so He had to punish them for their disobedience, but He still loved them. Sadly, they did not love Him in return. Ever since that time, just like Adam and Eve, everyone has done the same. We have all fallen short of God's glory. We have all hurt God by our selfish and sinful choices. *All* people are guilty of sin, Eiko—including you and me."

Eiko considered her friend's words before answering. "So it is a good thing that Jesus loves sinners because all of us are sinners. ..."

Sayuri's face lit up. "Exactly! God's love includes everybody. He still—even after all the hurt He receives—wants to have relationship with the people He made. We are here on earth because He created us. He gave us physical life, but His desire is to give us spiritual life. To show us how to do that, Jesus, God's only Son, came down from heaven to live among us. He taught everything the Father had shared with Him to those who would listen. Then He died on the Cross for us, taking our punishment so we could be set free from our sin and guilt. The Bible says Jesus had no sin, but He took everyone's sins upon Himself, upon His body. After three days in the tomb, He rose from the dead so that we, too, can live with Him forever in heaven after our days on earth are over. He saves all those who admit they are sinners and trust in Jesus as their Savior and Lord."

Eiko's heart seemed to be racing. "So is that why Christians like to put crosses on their cards?" She pulled out Hope's card and showed it to her friend. "I got this name card from someone on the way home from work."

"Oh, how nice!" Sayuri smiled, and her dark eyes seemed to glow. "It is important for Christians to remember Jesus' completed work on the Cross. A cross or a Bible verse helps to remind us of that great act of love. This verse is about friendship with Jesus. God wants you to hear this message." She smiled again. "That is two people, giving you the same message, in such a short time."

"I thought the very same thing," Eiko admitted. "Two people, with the same message... I will give it some more thought, Sayuri."

They sat quietly then, drinking another cup of ocha, until Sayuri broke the silence. "Eiko, I have been meaning to ask you something. How is your father? Has his condition changed any?"

The sad feelings threatened to return, as Eiko answered. "Well, actually, I just phoned my mother to ask. I am sad to say that his condition has not changed. He is still in a coma. My mother goes to see him every day and hopes he can feel her presence nearby."

"Would it be okay if I told my church about your father and asked them to pray for him?"

Eiko felt her eyes widen. "You mean, they would do that for my papa, even without me going to your church?"

Sayuri's smile was warm. "Sure, they will. They pray for anyone and everyone. It is part of the Christian life to talk to the Heavenly Father in prayer, about everything that concerns us and for everything we, or others, need."

Eiko was taken aback at her friend's kindness and generosity. "Arigatou! Thank you. Yes, please have your church pray for my father. I do not think my mother will mind, since I followed her instructions to go to the Buddhist temple and write out a prayer. I guess asking many gods is wiser."

Sayuri's smile faded, but her dark eyes telegraphed compassion. "That is not true. If it is the Heavenly Father whom you ask, that is all you need. He is the Creator of the universe, the One who holds everything together in this world.

When you ask Him, you do not need to ask any other gods. He has no equal. In fact, He gets jealous if we worship other gods. He wants all of our love, just as He has given us all of His by sending Jesus, His Only Son, to die for us."

"Oh, I am sorry." Eiko's voice cracked as she spoke. "I...I did not know."

Sayuri laid her hand on Eiko's arm. "Do not worry. I am happy to share the Truth with you. When you think about the Christian God, you have to think big!" Sayuri chuckled. "Matter of fact, there is a cute children's song that goes like this: 'My God is so *big*/ So strong and so mighty/ There's nothing my God can not do.[ii]

Eiko's voice was soft, as she asked, "So no prayer request is too hard for your God?"

"That is right," Sayuri reassured Eiko. "Remember, He is your God, too. He loved the entire world so much that He sent Jesus to *all* of us. Jesus came for you, too, Eiko."

Their dessert arrived, and they let the conversation go. Before long, Eiko and Sayuri said goodnight and headed home.

Once there, she reached over to her nightstand and pulled out the New Testament she had received at Mrs. Itoh's wake. Turning on the light, she opened the book randomly to Romans 5:11. Her eyes focused on the left side of the page, about halfway down, where she read the words aloud. "But that is not all; we rejoice because of what God has done through our Lord Jesus Christ, who has now made us God's friends."

If I did not know better, I might believe that God Himself opened the Bible to this page, so I would find this particular verse. Then

---

ii My God is So Big (Great)
    Words and Music by Ruth Harms Calkin
    ©Nuggets of Truth Publishing
    Used by permission.

she remembered the simple children's song that Sayuri had mentioned to her: "My God is so big/ So strong and so mighty/ There's nothing my God can not do." With that thought in mind, she laid the Bible down on the nightstand and soon fell into a deep, peaceful sleep.

On Monday morning, when Eiko arrived at work, she was pleased to see that Satoh seemed to be waiting for her. He smiled and held the door open for her so they could go in together. "Eiko, how are you?"

She smiled up at him. "Fine, thank you. And you?"

Satoh assured her he was doing well, then said, "I was wondering... Would you like to have lunch with me at our favorite noodle shop today?"

"Yes. That would be nice."

Satoh grinned. "See you then." He headed to the stairs, leaving her to catch the elevator.

The morning passed quickly, and Eiko soon found herself in the ramen shop with Satoh, happily slurping a hot, steamy bowl of ramen.

"This is delicious," Eiko exclaimed. "I was hungry for noodles today."

"I knew you would learn to like the taste of Tokyo ramen," Satoh teased.

Eiko grinned. "Sometime I hope you will go with me to Hokkaido to taste Hokkaido ramen. It is the best!"

Satoh shook his head, the light in his eyes still teasing her. "Aw, that is not fair. So you still have Hokkaido ramen as first place in your heart. I cannot believe it!"

"Satoh kun, be serious. Can we talk about your cousin's wedding?"

He shrugged. "Sure. Why not. What about it?"

"How did Aki become a Christian?" She watched Satoh's face closely as she spoke. "Was it because he fell in love with the pastor's daughter? Do you think he did it just for her? Or was it real?"

Satoh's lighthearted teasing look was gone, and his eyebrows were drawn together. "What is this all about, Eiko? Why are you so curious?"

"I just...wonder how it happens. You are close to your cousin, aren't you? Has he ever told you anything about his God?"

His frown deepened. "You know that Japanese do not like to talk about religion. It is private. It is nobody's business. So, no, he never really talked about it. All I know is that he hung around church a lot to see Yoko. He is so in love with her, he wants to be wherever she is."

"I see."

When she said no more, Satoh's expression softened. "I did give him a hard time, though—once or twice. He told me to quit because he really believed he had found something that made him feel whole. That is how he said it."

Eiko nodded slowly. "I think Aki is lucky to feel whole. It sounds like he is happy, not searching for anything, and that his needs are being met."

"I never really thought about it, myself," Satoh admitted. "Maybe I will ask him to explain it sometime."

"That would be nice. I would like to know, too."

When Satoh glanced at his watch, they realized it was time to get back to work before the lunch hour ended. Eiko was pleased that Satoh would consider asking his cousin about Christianity.

Maybe that means that Satoh, himself, wants to know more.... She was surprised at how the thought warmed her heart.

CHAPTER SEVEN

A s Eiko stepped out of the elevator on her floor, she saw Mr. Itoh waiting to enter. She had noticed he seemed a bit more relaxed these days. "Konnichiwa, Mr. Itoh," she said, with a slight lowering of her head to be respectful. He acknowledged her words with a slight nod and got on the elevator.

As she walked to her work station, she could imagine how lonely he must be without his beloved wife. The thought of her mother maybe having to live each day without her papa made Eiko's heart ache. It was bad enough for her mother to deal with her papa's hospitalization and the fact that, week to week, his condition remained the same. How much worse would it be if he passed on?

Before she could get too lost in such sad thoughts, Akiyama san, the kind lady that worked next to her, asked, "Did you see Mr. Itoh leaving our floor?"

Eiko nodded. "Yes, I did."

"And did you see the workman with him?"

Eiko paused. "Now that you mention it, yes, there did seem to be a man with him."

"I saw them standing together earlier, under the god-shelf in the corner. Mr. Itoh told him it needed to be removed. In its place, he wants to hang a Japanese calligraphy writing."

"Oh, I see," Eiko replied, though she really didn't. She did, however, wonder what the calligraphy writing would say.

The lady continued to discuss the subject. "Don't you think it will be bad luck for the company? That god-shelf has been there all the years I have worked here. It is such a shame that it has to come down. Things are going so well for the company. I am afraid for the future, aren't you?"

Eiko had heard stories like that since childhood, warnings about not angering the gods. She had never had any firsthand experience, but she certainly wouldn't want the gods to be angry with her family—especially now, since she wrote a prayer request for their help with her father. Eiko thought about the Buddhist altar in her parent's home in Sapporo, but they never had a Shinto god-shelf.

"I cannot really say. I do not know enough," Eiko admitted. "All I know is that I have got lots of work to do, and I had better get started."

Akiyama san smiled and nodded. "Of course. As do I."

On her way home from work, Eiko thought about stopping in at Mr. Sakamoto's store to ask him what he thought about the god-shelf coming down. *But not today,* she told herself. *I want to get home and fix something to eat.*

After eating supper and cleaning up, Eiko watched some TV news, warning of a typhoon that would hit the Tokyo area soon. She flipped off the TV and went to bed, but she couldn't fall asleep. Instead, she lay there, thinking about everything that had happened in the last few weeks. She remembered Hope's prayer for her papa, while she was visiting him in the hospital in Sapporo. The prayer, though brief, was warm and heartfelt. Hope's words had caused Eiko to feel hopeful and peaceful.

"It is funny," she mused aloud. "I had not thought about that prayer again until today. Now it has greater significance in my life. Creator God sent a Christian I had never met to say a prayer for my papa. This Christian God, or Creator God, as Sayuri refers to Him, is amazing. Now, through Sayuri's church, many prayers will be said for him to get well. This God is really so caring!"

Eiko's musings were interrupted then, as she heard the sounds of rain coming down in torrents. It had started quickly; she hoped everyone had time to get under a shelter.

The next morning, on her way to work, Eiko saw the mess the typhoon had made as it passed through. She carefully avoided the puddles and muddy patches on the sidewalks, and when she exited the train station and looked up, the lingering gray clouds still loomed

She had no sooner left the station and started walking toward her office than she heard music playing, just to the right of her. She looked in that direction and spotted a young Japanese lady, wearing a long skirt and vest. She had a lovely voice, which matched the soft sounds coming from her guitar. Eiko listened closely to the words—until someone tapped her on the shoulder. She turned to see Sayuri standing beside her.

"She is quite good," Eiko said. "It is a special song—so gentle and peaceful. She is singing in English, though, so I cannot understand the meaning."

Sayuri said, "It is the Lord's Prayer. The words are taken right from the Bible. Matter of fact, many churches say the Lord's Prayer in unison each week."

"Oh, yes! I did hear it being said at the church. It is very meaningful. I did not know it had been put to music," Eiko admitted.

"It is sung all over the world by Christians in their own languages."

As they turned their attention back to the woman who was singing, they noticed several people placing money in the young lady's open guitar case. They both reached into their purses and placed some of their own money in her case. Before she could begin another song, Eiko and Sayuri decided to walk on down the street toward the office.

"By the way," Sayuri said, "I called you last night, but you did not answer."

Eiko nodded. "I am not surprised. The storm messed up the phone lines, I think."

Sayuri nodded. "That is okay. I wanted to ask you something. The singles at our church are planning a retreat in the mountains soon. One of the girls cannot go, so there is room for one more. Would you like to go?"

Eiko was surprised at the invitation and wanted to know more about it. "How much does it cost, and when is it?"

"The cost is already taken care of. All you have to do is pay for your train fare. It starts at eight on Friday evening—not this coming Friday, but next Friday night—and goes until ten-thirty on Sunday morning.."

"That is nice of you to invite me." Eiko had been surprised at the invitation, but she was even more surprised to realize that she wanted to accept. "I think it might be something I would enjoy. But if it starts at seven, there will be no time to go home after work on Friday, if we want to make it in time."

"That is right," Sayuri agreed as they reached their destination and walked through the lobby toward the elevator. "We can bring our small clothes-bags to work with us and keep them under our desk. It will be cold this time of year in the mountains, so do not forget to pack a jacket."

Eiko smiled as she sat down at her desk and began organizing her work day. If she concentrated real hard on getting all of her work done with excellence, the ten days would go by more quickly.

When work ended for the day, Eiko ran into Satoh on the steps outside the office building.

He grinned when he saw her. "Hey, I am glad I ran into you. I have some news to tell you."

"What news?" Eiko asked, as she fell into step beside him.

"I have made plans to go see Aki and his wife next weekend, and I want you to go with me. We can ask him your questions about church and Christianity together."

Eiko's good mood melted away as she realized she couldn't accompany Satoh. "I am sorry, Satoh kun. I have something else planned that weekend. I cannot go with you."

Satoh stopped walking and looked down at her. She thought she saw hurt in his eyes, but perhaps it was only disappointment.

"Do you mind me asking what it is?" Satoh said. "I thought this would be important enough to override any other plans."

"I will be at a church retreat in the mountains."

"What?" Satoh's brow lifted, and it was obvious he wasn't pleased by the news. "What have you not told me?"

She opened her mouth to explain that she had just been invited that morning, but Satoh glanced at his watch and said, "I am sorry, Eiko, but I have to go. We can talk some other time."

Eiko watched as Satoh disappeared from view, confused by their brief meeting.

Later, Eiko lay on her bed, thinking about her encounter with Satoh. Why did he have to behave as he did? She was free to make her own plans, wasn't she? Of course, she was! They were not boyfriend and girlfriend, just friends. Yet she knew he had made those plans to visit his cousin with her in mind—to please her. Eiko wrestled with her decision to go on the singles' retreat with Sayuri's church, or to change her plans and go with Satoh. If she backed out now, Sayuri would be disappointed, and her friendship with Sayuri was more important to her than her friendship with Satoh.

"I did the right thing," Eiko said out loud "It was the best choice. Maybe I will have a chance to go with Satoh to his cousin's place another time—if he still wants me to go anywhere with him."

The highlight of Eiko's week had been the dinner with the Sakamotos. She enjoyed Mrs. Sakamoto's wonderful cooking and the opportunity to talk with all of them about their interests and activities. It also kept her from thinking so much about Satoh's disappointment.

The week before the retreat had passed quickly, without seeing Satoh. Eiko tried not to think about it, as she and Sayuri boarded the train for the mountains.

The train ride up the mountain was pleasant, though much of it was in darkness. The small towns along the way provided only a few flickers of light in the view out the window. Most of the passengers sat quietly as the train headed for its destination. Sayuri and Eiko spoke in low voices so as not to disturb the others.

"Are you looking forward to the retreat?" Sayuri asked.

"Yes…even though I am a little nervous about meeting people," Eiko admitted.

Sayuri's smile was encouraging. "Everyone is really nice. I think you will feel at ease right away. This is a good opportunity to make some new friends."

Finally, the train pulled slowly into the quaint mountain station. The two friends got their bags down from the shelf above them and gathered their things as they moved toward the doors and out into the starlit night. After exiting the station, they quickly pulled out their jackets and put them on. They shivered a bit, as they waited in line for a taxi to take them to the retreat center down the road.

After paying the taxi fare, they headed to the registration desk to get their room assignment. A young man named Wada, dressed in jeans and a brown plaid shirt, greeted them.

"Sayuri san, good evening! I see you made it. This must be Eiko san. Nice to meet you."

Eiko bowed slightly to acknowledge Wada's greeting, while Sayuri introduced him as the singles' coordinator at church. "He is the one responsible for planning the retreat."

"I had help from the others," he confessed. "After you check into your room and get settled, you will find most of us hanging out in meeting room one-oh-seven, down the hall, near the cafeteria. Our program will start at eight."

"Oh, that only gives us twenty minutes," Eiko said, glancing at her watch.

"That will be plenty of time," Sayuri assured her. "Let us go find our room right away."

Once in their room, the ladies went to the closet and took out bedding to make up two futons on the *tatami*, or rice mat, floor.

"Old-style sleeping arrangements, I see," Eiko observed. "I have not slept on a futon in a long time."

Sayuri nodded. "Yes, western-style beds are popular now—especially for our age and younger. But it is fun sleeping the traditional way once again. I believe futons were designed for the most comfort and ease. I heard this place also has rooms with beds, but the room fee is more expensive. For our purposes, the singles decided to stay more cheaply."

"Since our room does not include a private bath, we can go to the traditional ladies' ofuro down the hall, right?" Eiko asked.

"Yes. That's the best way to rest well...a deep, hot bath and a soft, warm futon. After our long day, it will be wonderful!"

As the ladies walked out and closed the door behind them, they looked at their watches. It was already eight as they walked down the hallway and headed over to the meeting room.

"*Konbanwa, minna* san. Good evening, everyone!" Wada called out. "We are so glad you are here for the weekend retreat. We have a guest with us this weekend. Everyone, meet Eiko san. She works at the same office as Sayuri san. Sayuri san, thank you for bringing her."

Sayuri acknowledged his comments with a nod, as she and Eiko took their seats.

"Okay, we are ready to start," Wada said. "Come to the stage, band members. Let us sing for a while." They spent the next half-hour singing contemporary-style music with Christian words. Eiko found the new music intriguing. It seemed to reach into her heart and stir up feelings of peace and joy.

Next, the speaker came up front and took the microphone in his hand. "Hello, everyone. My name is Masahiro. For the remaining few minutes, I would like to share with you how I became a Christian. I have always loved nature, since Japan is blessed with beauty all around. We have mountains, lakes, trees, birds, insects, and flowers, all unique and special. As a little boy, I collected rocks that I found while hiking. Another hobby I had was capturing beetles each summer."

He paused for a moment to smile at his audience, then went on. "I often wondered how this beautiful nature came to be. Some people I asked said that nature has its own wisdom and created itself. Others said they did not know. But when I was in junior high, I met a Japanese professor who told me that a very special Creator was responsible for all of it, a Creator who loves everything He created, both large and small. For example, He loves whales just as much as minnows, cranes as well as sparrows, Mt. Fuji just as much as Sheep Hill, and oceans as well as tiny brooks."

Eiko was drawn to the warmth in the man's words, and she listened intently.

"I wanted to learn more about this wonderful Creator, so the professor explained to me that the Creator was most proud of His last creation. He made man first out of the dust of the earth and breathed life into his nostrils. Then He put the man into a deep sleep and made a woman from the man's rib, to be a helper-partner to him. I thought that made much more sense than the idea that humans came from monkeys, although it is true that we do like to be silly and imitate others."

The group laughed, and Eiko joined in.

Masahiro continued. "The professor also told me that this Creator's name is Almighty God, and His one and only Son, Jesus, was there with Him when creation took place. He spoke everything into being, and it happened just as He said. I was surprised when the professor said Creator God desires relationship with each person. He wants to be our Heavenly Father."

He paused for a moment, as Eiko pondered his last words.

"When the professor finished his talk," he continued, "he asked for people who were interested in a personal relationship with Jesus to come and speak with him. I was one of the first ones to make it down to the front. That night I became a Christian, a child of God."

Glancing at his wristwatch, Masahiro said, "Well, I see I have used up my time, but if you have any questions, please talk to me anytime during the retreat."

Wada san came back up to the stage and asked everyone to bow their heads for a closing prayer. "Almighty God," he began, "thank You for your beautiful creation. Thank You for making people, and for the life You have given each one of us. Help us to feel special and unique because we have You as our Creator, and your precious Son, Jesus, as our Savior and Lord. Thank You for helping us get to know You better. Your love for each of us is changing us from the inside out. Please make this weekend one we will not forget. Amen."

Slowly, the small crowd got up from their seats and went to stand around the refreshment table. "Would you like some hot chocolate?" a young lady asked Eiko.

"Yes, please," she answered, pleasantly surprised by the warmth and friendliness of the group.

The young lady smiled and handed a steaming cup to Eiko. "My name is Miyo. My friends call me Michan. I am glad you are here."

"I am glad, too, Michan," Eiko replied. "It has been very interesting so far."

After her ofuro, Eiko went to her room and got under the warm, comfortable futon covers. She was asleep before Sayuri made it back to the room.

❧ ❧ ❧

On Saturday morning, Eiko woke up early, got dressed, and went for a walk before breakfast. She made it to a high place by following the trail behind the retreat center. Looking out over the small valley town to the tall mountains beyond, she watched the sun make its majestic entrance to welcome the day. She heard a variety of birds singing their own unique songs to add to the new day's welcome.

Overwhelmed by the beauty that surrounded her, Eiko's barely audible voice whispered, "So Almighty God made all of this...?"

"Yes, He did," spoke a voice to the left, slightly behind her. "It is nice to see that someone else enjoys sunrises as much as I do."

Eiko turned to see Masahiro standing next to her.

"I am from Hokkaido," Eiko said, "so I miss the beautiful landscapes during the four seasons. I guess living in a metropolis like Tokyo eventually dulls the senses. I do not see stars at night or sunrises from my neighborhood apartment. But I am blessed to know that they are there, even without seeing them."

Masahiro nodded. "That is like faith in God—you believe He exists because you experience His love and salvation personally. You know He is there, interacting in your life, even without seeing Him."

"Well, I do not know He is there, truthfully," Eiko admitted. "I like the idea, but it still seems strange that He has not shown Himself to me, my family, or most of my friends."

Masahiro smiled. "God's Word, the Bible, says He has already shown Himself to everyone. The New Century Version of Psalm 19:1 says it this way: 'The heavens declare the glory of God, and the skies announce what his hands have made.' "

"Then why do we Japanese worship many other gods?"

"I would guess that it is by choice. Yet there have been those throughout our nation's history who chose to believe in Almighty God and trust in His only son, Jesus, as their personal Savior and Lord. That history includes stories of brave Christians, including traditional warriors, the samurai, who were martyred for their faith in Jesus Christ."

"I do not remember ever hearing that in history class at school."

"Yes, I know. It is shocking to hear, but true," Masahiro assured her.

The clanging of a loud bell pierced the quiet of the morning skies, and they looked down at the source of the ringing.

"That is coming from the dining room," Masahiro explained. "It is breakfast time."

They hurried down the path to the clearing below, where the retreat center nestled in a beautiful meadow. Bright autumn leaves, with red, orange, and golden hues, glistened with the morning dew in the new light of sunrise. Eiko took a deep breath of fresh air as she approached the line, waiting for the dining room to open.

A sense of peace flooded Eiko's heart, as she allowed her mind to whisper, *Arigatou gozaimasu for Your beautiful creation, Almighty God!*

Sayuri tried to get Eiko's attention then, as she waved to her. "Eiko, over here!"

Happy to see Sayuri and the others from the church, Eiko joined them in line.

"You are up early. You could not sleep?" one of the young ladies asked.

Eiko smiled. "Actually, I woke up early and took a short hike up the mountain to see the sunrise."

"Sounds nice. Did you get there in time?" Sayuri asked.

"I did. The timing was perfect."

Masahiro voiced his agreement, as he, too, joined up with the group.

The day went by quickly, filled with small-group time, worship time, which included a message and music, free time at the nearby lake, three delicious meals, and a fun night of group games. The singles were all friendly and seemed stress-free, while enjoying their time together.

And then another day had passed. Eiko and Sayuri turned off the lights, as they each got under their futon covers that night.

"Sayuri, thanks for suggesting I come with you to the retreat. It is even better than I thought it would be." Eiko stopped, feeling her cheeks get warm. "I am so sorry. That sounded bad."

Sayuri smiled "No. I understand what you are saying, Eiko. That is an honest answer. I am glad that you have been surprised in a good way."

After a sound sleep, they were awakened as the morning light peeked through a small opening in the curtains.

"Eiko, we need to hurry," Sayuri said as she checked her watch. "Breakfast is in twenty minutes, and we are supposed to have our luggage down in the lobby before our meeting starts."

Eiko jumped up, folded her futon, and put it in the closet. She gathered the sheets and put them outside the door to their room, as they had been instructed. Sayuri did the same. With only a few items needing to be repacked in each of their bags, they were dressed and down in the lobby, smiles on their faces, with a couple of minutes to spare.

Some members of their group, who got to the lobby a bit earlier, greeted them. "Ohayou," Michan and some others chimed in. Some looked sleepy, no doubt from staying up to talk through the night. Others looked energetic to begin the new day.

Then many in the group began to greet one another with the words from Psalm 118:24: "This is the day that the Lord has made. Let us rejoice and be glad today."

Eiko recognized the words as one of the scripture songs the group loved to sing. Her heart seemed to soar as she listened to the words and then whispered in agreement, "This is the day the Lord has made. I will rejoice and be glad in it."

The aroma of steamed rice and cooked fish made Eiko realize how hungry she was at that moment. Someone from the kitchen brought out miso soup on a cart, and the meal was complete.

One of the young ladies, whose name was Hanako, said a short prayer, and then everyone started eating. Eiko was thankful for the traditional breakfast. Most days, at her apartment, she only had time for a piece of toast before leaving for work.

The retreat program was scheduled to end at 10:30. After breakfast, they gathered in their meeting room for singing and a message. Then they broke up into small groups for prayer. Most of the prayer requests involved problems at work or relationship troubles. A few asked prayer for health-related needs.

Eiko's thoughts turned to her papa's medical problems. While trying to decide if she should say anything, Hanako spoke up. "Eiko, we have been praying at our church for your papa's health. Is he any better?"

Eiko blinked in surprise, and then she remembered Sayuri asking for permission to share her papa's condition with her church. "I want to thank everyone at church who is praying," Eiko said. "My papa is in a coma, and the doctors are not sure what caused his condition, but they think it was a stroke from overwork. The last few times I talked on the phone with my mother, she sounded so tired that our conversations were very short. Please pray for her to get the rest she needs. Pray for my brother to go to the hospital more to give my mother a break. And, please, continue praying that my papa will wake up and be okay."

Hanako then asked, "How can we pray for you personally, Eiko?"

Eiko hadn't considered her own needs for prayer. Realizing that Hanako was showing concern for her, she thought for a minute and then said, "Please pray that I will stay strong for my family and not get depressed."

Hanako started the prayer time, and others took turns. Everyone's requests were prayed for with kindness and concern. Eiko's heart was warmed when she heard the prayers for herself and her family.

If only she could have the same confidence in Creator God that the others did. She wanted to believe that He was listening and would help her in ways she couldn't even imagine at that moment. But time would tell...and she was willing to wait.

CHAPTER EIGHT

Eiko unlocked the door to her apartment and stepped inside. The trip home from the retreat had been very enjoyable. Most of the participants had stopped in the quaint mountain town to do some window shopping and eat at a local restaurant before getting on the train back to Tokyo.

Eiko gathered up a small load of laundry and put it in her tiny washing machine. She watched some TV until the clothes were done, then she draped everything on the special portable clothes rack that she kept under her bed when she wasn't using it.

With that done, Eiko decided to walk down to the Sakamotos' place to see how they were doing. While at the mountain resort, she had purchased some specialty breads for them.

"Konnichiwa," she said, when she spotted Mr. Sakamoto closing up his shop. "How are you doing?"

Mr. Sakamoto smiled. "I am doing well, thank you. And welcome back! How was it?"

"It was really nice to be in the mountains. The leaves have started to change color, and I really enjoyed my time away from the city. I guess I miss Hokkaido more than I want to admit," Eiko confessed.

"Me, too!" Mr. Sakamoto agreed.

"I brought you something" she said. "Some specialty breads for your family to enjoy. Is Mrs. Sakamoto home?"

He nodded. "Yes, she is. Let us go on up together. As you can see, I just closed my shop for the day." As they climbed the stairs, Mr. Sakamoto called out, "Mama, Eiko chan is here for a visit!"

As they opened the door and stepped inside, Mrs. Sakamoto's voice could be heard, talking on the telephone in the kitchen.

"Let us surprise her, Eiko chan," Mr. Sakamoto suggested with a smile. "Follow me into the living room."

Eiko left her shoes off in the genkan and went inside.

Mrs. Sakamoto soon finished her conversation and came into the living room, her face lighting up the moment she spotted her company. "Oh, Eiko chan, what a surprise! You are back. It is good to see you. I am sorry I was on the phone."

"That is quite all right," Eiko assured her. "I just wanted to come by and give you this souvenir from the mountain retreat, where I spent the weekend. It is a favorite of the locals in that area."

Eiko handed the wrapped box to Mrs. Sakamoto, who received it humbly.

"Arigatou, Eiko chan," she said as she opened the package. "You really should not have spent your money on us."

"I am happy she did," Mr. Sakamoto teased. "I love that type of bread."

Mr. Sakamoto thanked Eiko as Mrs. Sakamoto went into the kitchen to make some green tea to serve with their treat.

"Did you go to the mountains with friends?" Mr. Sakamoto inquired.

Eiko nodded. "My friend from work, Sayuri, invited me to go with some friends of hers."

"Was it a church retreat?"

Eiko lifted her eyebrows in surprise. "Yes, it was. How did you guess?"

Mr. Sakamoto grinned. "Well, that area has long been known as a wonderful place for spiritual retreats. You look happy. Was it good for your spirit?"

"It was. I feel ... happy. I think it was just what I needed. Have you ever been on a church retreat, Mr. Sakamoto?"

"I was invited to one when I was in college," he explained, "but it did not work out for me to go along, although my best friend went. It caused my friend to give up things we enjoyed doing together, like drinking to relax at the end of the day. After the retreat, he would read his Bible and pray instead of drinking, saying it always made him feel better."

"Did that make you want to believe, too, seeing how his life had changed?"

Mr. Sakamoto's shoulders drooped a bit, and the smile faded from his face. "I am ashamed to admit that I worried more about my friends' reactions. Also, I did not want to have to give up alcohol." He sighed. "There were times that alcohol was my best friend, but later I got very ill and the doctor said I had to quit. So I did. I learned from my experience that most people drink to forget their troubles, without thinking about all of the troubles and harm alcohol does to themselves and those they love."

"What did you quit, dear?" Mrs. Sakamoto asked, coming into the room with some green tea and a plateful of raisin bread slices, croissants, and a few other choices of bread that Eiko had brought them. Mrs. Sakamoto set a little plate to the side of each ocha cup. Not waiting for her husband to answer, she went back to the kitchen for some orange marmalade and strawberry jam. "Please help yourself, Eiko chan," she said, as she reentered the room. "You say you were away at a mountain retreat. How was it?"

"It was very nice; thank you for asking. I met some friendly people my age, and the mountain views reminded me of Hokkaido. It was relaxing to get away from the concrete city."

Mrs. Sakamoto smiled, and Eiko saw a twinkle in her dark eyes as she spoke. "Any special young men there? Did you talk with any of them?"

"About one-third of the group were young men." Eiko shrugged. "They were okay. I did have an interesting conversation with a young man named Masahiro, who graduated from college seven years ago. He truly loves the beauty and diversity in nature."

"Yes, those mountains are pure heaven to nature lovers," Mrs. Sakamoto agreed. "I do believe that people who honor the gods of the forest are more likely to receive the gifts the forest gives."

Eiko paused a moment before continuing. "Well, actually, Masahiro san said he worships Creator God. Sometimes he calls Him Almighty God. He said knowing the Creator is amazing and wonderful. He said it takes less faith to believe in a big God, who created everything, than in lots of little gods, who make only one thing, such as a tree, or a river, or the stars."

Mrs. Sakamoto's face registered her surprise. "Is that young man a foreigner? Surely, he could not be Japanese!"

Eiko thought for a minute about how she should answer. She didn't want to sound rude, but she wanted to share her opinion. While she was still pondering this, Mr. Sakamoto came to her rescue.

"Wife, what are you saying? Japanese can, and do, have lots of opinions. How can you say a particular opinion is Japanese or foreign? Japanese think for themselves."

"But we Japanese stick together and stay true to the wishes of our ancestors," his wife argued.

"Everyone there was Japanese, Mrs. Sakamoto," Eiko interjected.

Mr. Sakamoto gave his wife a stern look, and she quickly changed the subject. "These are delicious breads," she said with a smile. "The boys will love them, too, when they get home."

Eiko was happy to pursue another topic. "How are they doing?"

Mrs. Sakamoto beamed as she answered. "They are fine—just so busy, what with going to school, helping their father at the store, and participating in their clubs. Sunday is the day for their school clubs. They should be back soon."

"And I should be leaving to get ready for work tomorrow," Eiko said. "Thank you for the delicious cup of green tea."

Mrs. Sakamoto smiled and nodded. "You are welcome, Eiko chan. Please come back when you have more time."

Mr. Sakamoto walked her to the door. "Eiko chan, I think you are on the right path. Do not worry what others say. My advice is to follow your heart, wherever it leads."

Eiko was pleased with Mr. Sakamoto's encouragement. "Thank you for your kind words. They mean a lot to me."

With a quick goodbye, she stepped outside and began her short walk home. *Yes, I must follow my heart….*

The street was quiet as she walked home. She could hear the phone ringing in her apartment, as she slid the key into the door. Once inside, she locked the door behind her and reached for the receiver.

Her mother's voice greeted her as soon as she put the phone to her ear. "Eiko?"

Alarm bells began to ring in Eiko's ears. "Mother, you sound too quiet. Are you okay?"

The woman's voice cracked, and Eiko could hear the tears in her voice. "Eiko, Papa is dead."

"What?" Eiko was certain she hadn't heard her mother correctly. It couldn't possibly be true that her beloved papa was dead. "I cannot hear you," she said. "What did you say?"

Her mother moaned. "I do not know what to say, other than your papa is gone."

"Gone?" Eiko caught her breath, feeling her heart begin to race. "When did it happen? Why didn't you let me know his condition was worse? You know I would have come."

"Eiko, please forgive me," she said, her voice weak and shaky. "I did not know. No one knew. He died today."

"How? What happened?"

"The machines alerted the nurses at their station. He died peacefully."

Eiko let out a sob. "But why now? He was supposed to get better!"

They waited in silence for a moment, as if neither knew what to say to the other.

"I should come home," Eiko said at last.

"Yes," her mother agreed. "Papa would want you here now, as he would have wanted you to be here when he died. But it could not be helped."

"Is ... older brother with you now?"

"Yes. And so is my friend."

Eiko was relieved to know that her mother wasn't alone. "Good. Okay. I will see you as soon as possible."

As she hung up the phone and flopped down on the bed, a flood of tears burst forth from her breaking heart. Tomorrow she would have to figure things out; tonight she wanted only to think about how much she would miss her sweet papa.

She awoke the next morning with a headache. Rising slowly, she realized she must call her workplace to let them know she wouldn't be coming in. Immediately, she thought of Sayuri, who might be able to tell her what to do. Dialing Sayuri's number, Eiko hoped she would already be up.

"Moshi moshi," Sayuri answered on the first ring.

"Sayuri san? This is Eiko. I am sorry to call you this early in the morning, but I need your help."

"What is it, Eiko san? How can I help you?"

She took a deep breath, determined to get through the phone call without breaking down. "Papa passed away yesterday. I...I got the news last night. I need to return to Hokkaido for the wake and the funeral. I do not know who to tell at the office."

"Oh, Eiko san, I am so sorry to hear this! I will help any way I can. I believe you need to call your supervisor first. Do you have her contact information?"

"Yes, but she is on vacation, and I do not know who else to tell."

"Do not worry. I will talk to Mr. Itoh's secretary and tell her."

Relief and gratitude washed over Eiko. "Arigatou, Sayuri. I really appreciate your help."

After a brief pause, Sayuri asked, "Are you going to be okay, Eiko? I know you must be very sad to lose your papa. I will pray for you as you travel to Hokkaido to be with your family. Please remember that Almighty God feels your sadness and wants to show you His love and comfort."

"I will remember," Eiko promised.

"Take care, Eiko."

"Okay. Thanks. I will phone you while I am there."

After ending that call, Eiko called the airline to arrange a flight as soon as possible. She was grateful that her papa had wanted her to have a credit card, which she could use in emergencies, while she lived in Tokyo. Her mother had helped her get one from their bank, and it would come in handy now, as this certainly was an emergency.

She took care of her travel details, then got a shower and packed her bag before remembering two other calls she needed to make—one to the Sakamotos and one to Satoh kun.

"Sakamoto san," she said when Mr. Sakamoto answered the phone. "I just wanted to let you know that Papa passed away last night." She swallowed the lump that seemed to have taken up residence in her throat. "I am going back to Hokkaido to be with my family."

The man's sympathy and concern were evident in his voice. "So sad to hear, Eiko chan. Really too bad. Are you going to be gone a long time?"

"No. I will be back after everything is settled. Maybe two weeks, I think."

"Eiko, is there anything you need? We want to help if we can."

"I cannot think of anything."

"How will you get to the airport?"

"I will take the train."

"Do you have time to stop by the house on your way to the train station?"

She thought for a moment. "I guess I can, but only for a few minutes."

"Yes, of course. I understand."

"See you in a little while then."

She hung up and thought again of the other call she wanted to make—to Satoh. But a glance at her watch told her there was no time. She would try to call him while she was gone.

Eiko managed to stop by the Sakamotos' place and still get to the airport, check-in, and board her flight in time. She shoved her small bag under the seat in front of her, and as she sank into her seat and buckled her seatbelt, she concentrated on the engine noise, as the plane waited in line for takeoff. She clutched the armrests, as the plane ascended, her sadness over her father's death leaving her tired and confused. When the flight attendant came by to offer her something to drink, Eiko was still lost in her thoughts. She remembered Sayuri's kindness in telling the boss's secretary about her papa's death, and the kindness of the Sakamoto family in presenting her a money envelope to use for funeral expenses.

The flight attendant repeated her offer of refreshments, and Eiko managed to get out the words, "Ocha, please." Once the attendant had delivered the tea, Eiko forced herself to take a sip and to nibble on the sweet-bean pastry the attendant had left with her.

In slightly over an hour, the plane landed at Chitose Airport. The flight attendant on the speaker phone thanked everyone for flying with them and added, "If Hokkaido is your home, welcome back, and everyone please enjoy your stay. We hope to serve you again soon."

Eiko walked quickly through the terminal and past the baggage claim area to the arrival lobby, where she saw her brother waiting for her. As she hurried into his welcoming embrace, tears fell from her cheeks as fast as she could wipe them away.

Yu took her small bag from her. "The car is parked nearby. Let us go home," he said, as he put his arm around her shoulder and led her out to the parking lot.

On the ride home, Eiko heard the details of her papa's last few minutes of life, as well as all the preparations that had already been finalized for the wake and funeral. She also learned that her papa's eldest brother and mother had already arrived and were staying at their house.

"The wake is scheduled for Thursday evening, and the funeral is on Friday morning," Yu informed her. "It will be at the local community hall. Between the two ceremonies, a total of several hundred people are expected to attend, so that seemed the best place to have it."

Eiko didn't hear anything else he might have said. She leaned her head back and let her body go limp against the cushioned seat, as they made their way to their two-story home in Sapporo. Eiko and her brother rode in silence during the forty-five minute trip. Arriving at home, they entered the house and greeted their mother and relatives, who were busy preparing a late lunch for them.

After all the greetings and condolences, Eiko headed up to her room. As she opened her door, the family's Siamese cat ran in and jumped up on her bed. Eiko laid down on the bed and stroked the cat's fur. "Did you miss me, Kiku?"

The cat meowed, as she purred softly. Eiko's body felt so tired and heavy, and within minutes, she was fast asleep. She later learned that her mother had come to check on her and to tell her lunch was ready, but she didn't have the heart to wake her.

The day of the wake arrived, and Eiko's mother asked her to visit an elderly friend of their family, who lived in a retirement home across town. The friend had called, saying she was unable to attend the wake and funeral but wanted to give money to help with the flower costs. Everyone else in Eiko's family had errands that needed to be done before the evening wake, so the responsibility fell to Eiko. Her mother insisted Eiko do something with a friend afterward, until the others returned home.

Obediently, Eiko called an old high-school friend, but she wasn't at home. She tried a neighborhood friend too, but she was at *juku*, cram school, studying for the important tests she had to take soon. Eiko was disappointed, but she decided to take the spending money her mother had offered her and do something on her own after visiting with the elderly family friend.

She rode the train and then walked several blocks to the lady's assisted-living facility. As she entered the place, she noticed the large, bright, cheery room, where several elderly people had already gathered in anticipation of some event. Looking around, she noticed a poster that mentioned a special choir concert that day. Eiko's mother had arranged for the friend to meet Eiko in this large area. She spotted their family friend, Fumiko san, and waved to her. Immediately the woman's face lit up with awareness, as Eiko approached.

"Eiko chan, it has been awhile, hasn't it? How are you doing?" The woman's eyes seemed filmy, no doubt from cataracts, but it was obvious that her memory was firmly intact. "It is such a sad time for you, and I am so sorry, Eiko chan. I know what it is like to lose a family member to death. It is not easy now, but it will get easier. Life has to go on. That is why I am here."

Eiko nodded in agreement, as tears bit her eyes. She sat down in a chair beside Fumiko san and waited for her to speak again. The woman reached in her pants pocket and pulled out the special money envelope for the funeral. She handed it to Eiko and requested that she give it to her mother. Eiko assured her that she would do it as soon as she returned home. "My family thanks you for your kindness," she said. "You are a dear friend to all of us."

Eiko was about to stand up to leave, when the woman laid her hand on Eiko's arm. "Eiko chan, do you have forty-five minutes to stay and listen to a guest choir? They will be singing to us this morning."

It was obvious the woman didn't want Eiko to leave. "The group is already here," she said, "practicing in another room. It starts in five minutes. I would love for you to stay. Please stay, Eiko chan. Besides, listening to music always gives me such peace and joy. Maybe you could use a little of that, too. What do you think?"

Eiko thought briefly about her plans for the rest of the afternoon, but decided it was more important to stay for the music. "Sure," she said. "It is okay. I will be happy to stay."

The guest choir came into the room and stood in two rows, facing the crowd that had gathered to listen to the concert. The pianist, who was off to the side, with her back to the audience, began playing before anyone realized she had come in. The songs were beautiful, the words pleasant, and the tunes comforting. At the end, the director thanked everyone for listening and appreciating the music. Then he said, "The reason the choir sings is to praise Almighty God, who sent His one and only Son, Jesus, into the world to be our Savior and Friend." Turning back to face the choir, he led them as they sang, "What a Friend We Have in Jesus."

The elderly nodded their heads, perhaps having heard it in the Christian churches that flourished after the war, when the Good News of Jesus Christ was heard by many Japanese for the first time. They clapped politely as the choir finished. Then the retirement home spokesperson invited everyone to stay for juice and *osembe*, rice crackers with different flavors.

Eiko soon said goodbye to her family friend and headed toward the main doors, passing by the piano on her way out. The pianist turned around at just that moment and looked up. "Eiko san? What a surprise to see you here!" Hope Tanner grinned. "This is my church group. How did you end up here today?"

Eiko couldn't believe it! Only Almighty God could have brought Hope to this place at this time so they would run into each other. The word "amazing" came to mind, and when Hope asked if Eiko had time to go to lunch with her, she gladly accepted. Eiko even offered to pay for the meal, planning to use the money her mother had given her. Hope said goodbye to her church friends and let them know she wouldn't be returning to the church with them.

On the way to the restaurant, Eiko told Hope why she was in Sapporo. Even though she hadn't known Hope long, Eiko felt safe talking with her. She felt that Hope listened with a caring heart, as Eiko tearfully recounted the details of the past few days. As they entered the ramen shop, the young ladies were quickly seated at a table near the kitchen. Eiko watched the busy chefs fill the orders with great speed. Within a few minutes, their orders of ramen and gyouza were brought to their table.

"I have missed Hokkaido ramen," Eiko admitted, as she finished her first bite. "My friend Satoh takes me to his favorite Tokyo ramen shop, and I have learned to enjoy the flavor, but Hokkaido ramen is better. I guess it is what you grow up eating that is always your favorite."

"Well, not always," Hope said with a smile. "I prefer Hokkaido ramen more than the chicken noodle soup in the USA, which is what I grew up eating."

Eiko smiled. "What else do you like about living in Japan?"

"Well, I love the four seasons in Hokkaido. Autumn is gorgeous, with the colorful leaves and the bike-riding. Winter is beautiful, with the snow and skiing. Spring is so lovely, with the flowers and hiking trails. And, of course, summer is pleasant and perfect for enjoying soft-serve ice cream, made at dairy farms in the area."

"So true," Eiko said with admiration, thinking that her new friend had summed up Hokkaido's seasons perfectly.

"Soon I must return to the USA," Hope said. "When Christmas comes, my two-year assignment will end. I plan to fly back to the States on December twenty-fourth, Christmas Eve."

"Are you sad that it is over? What will you do back in America?"

"I want to get a job and save money to come back here," Hope answered. "I will miss the people who have been a part of my life here in Sapporo. God has been so good to me while I've been here. He has blessed me with everything I've needed in my church family. They have loved me with God's love, and I've learned to love Japan because of them."

Eiko nodded. "I am glad you like Japan. Church people seem nice. I recently went to a young people's retreat in the mountains with a friend from work. I was nervous, since it was my first experience with a church group, but I had a nice time."

Hope beamed, and her hazel eyes danced. "That's great, Eiko san! I'm so glad you were able to go. God wants you to know how much He loves you. Did you feel His love for you during that time?"

Eiko nodded again. "At the retreat, I learned about Almighty God, the Creator of the universe. I learned that

He wants people to worship Him, instead of worshiping His creation in nature."

"That's right. He created people to have relationship with Him."

Eiko paused for a moment, then said, "Before the retreat, I went to a Christian wake at a church and heard that Jesus is a friend of sinners. A soloist sang a song called 'What a Friend We Have in Jesus.' It was tender, and it touched my heart in a strange way. Today those memories returned as your choir sang the same song."

"I remember you telling me about that, Eiko. It happened about the same time I met you for the second time on the train platform in Tokyo and gave you my name card. It had a Bible verse printed on it. Did you notice?"

Eiko smiled. "Yes. I read your Bible verse and liked it very much. I was beginning to think that Jesus was my Friend, but then my beloved papa died. Now I do not know what to think. My friend's church was praying for him to get well, but that did not happen. Papa dying does not exactly show God's love for me."

"Eiko, I wouldn't give up on God just yet," Hope said as she finished off the last gyouza. "God is always loving. Sometimes we don't understand *how* He is loving, especially when sad things happen to us. The Bible says that He shows His love to us by never leaving us alone. He is always with us, in sad times and happy times."

"Why is it that God does not heal everyone who gets prayed for?" Eiko asked.

Hope leaned forward and laid her hand on Eiko's arm. "It's because He has a master plan. We must believe that He is always working things out for our good. That requires faith, and faith pleases God. Prayer softens our hearts, so that we can accept His answers to our requests."

Eiko raised her eyebrows, a bit surprised and puzzled, too. "Oh?"

Hope continued. "In Heavenly Father's timing, we will experience His love for us, as He helps us through tough times and brings us into times of joyful blessing. I have had many experiences like this. My love for God keeps growing and growing, as I learn more and more about His love for me."

Eiko felt hesitant. "Well, maybe I need to wait and see before I decide to have faith."

"Faith is a gift from God, Eiko. He knocks at our heart's door and waits for us to open it before He comes in to be our Savior and Lord. He forgives us for our unbelief, as we confess that Jesus Christ is God's one and only Son, who took our place of punishment and shame on the Cross, even though He did no wrong. He is the spotless Lamb of God, who died and rose again on the third day, so that we could live free and forgiven, in right relationship with Almighty God, and receive His blessings in Christ Jesus forever."

It was almost too much to absorb. Eiko glanced at her watch. She was surprised at how quickly the time had passed. "I had better head home now. Thanks for suggesting lunch. It is my gift today. My mother told me to have lunch with a friend, since the others in my family were busy with errands this afternoon. I guess she did not want me to be alone."

"I'm glad God worked it out so I was the friend you had lunch with. I enjoyed our conversation. I will be praying for you and your family tonight at the wake and at the funeral tomorrow."

Eiko thanked her friend, paid the cashier, and walked out of the restaurant with Hope.

"What a beautiful blue sky," Hope commented, gazing upward. "No clouds in sight. Definitely nihonbare!" She waved goodbye, then climbed into a taxi.

Eiko waved back, watching the cab pull away. Then she turned and walked to the bus stop on the corner. She was still thinking about Hope's comment. How did Hope know about nihonbare? *I wish I could embrace the beautiful sky blue, too,* Eiko mused, *but today my thoughts are focused on the clouds I am experiencing inside of me.*

In a few minutes, she boarded the bus to head for home.

CHAPTER NINE

Eiko felt uncomfortable in her seat on the first row in the community hall, where friends and family gathered Thursday morning for her papa's funeral. She had made it through the wake the previous night, and now this, too, would soon be over.

Her mind wandered while the bright orange-robed Buddhist priests finished their chants. Looking at the photo of her father on the altar, with so many chrysanthemums on either side, made Eiko long to be at home, sitting in Papa's favorite chair, looking at the happy family photo that was taken last Christmas. Papa loved Christmas, and in recent years, he enjoyed having a family party with presents on December 23rd, which happened to be a national holiday, set aside to celebrate Emperor Akihito's birthday. Then Papa would take the family out to eat on Christmas Eve. The 23rd was the only holiday he would request off from work, saying his company needed him the rest of the time. He had been so overworked for the last two years that he hadn't had much time at home with Eiko and her brother. He was loyal to his company and his boss—normally an admirable trait, but right now one that squeezed her heart with pain.

Eiko's mother pointed out the large group of workers from the company, who had attended the wake last night and were also present this morning. Eiko noticed the many faces of neighbors and friends of their family, who had come to pay their respects. Her papa had been loved by a lot of people.

After the funeral, the family and close friends went to the crematorium to wait for the ashes and to have lunch— which consisted of catered bereavement obentous, paid for by the family and served in a special room with a large rice mat, low tables, and *zabuton* square cushions for sitting. While they waited and ate, Eiko's mother pulled out a few small envelopes from her purse and showed them to Eiko.

"What are these?" Eiko asked.

"Cards from people, or companies, who sent flowers for your father's wake and funeral. I do not recognize the names, and neither does your brother."

Eiko looked at the first card. It read, "From Eiko's friends at the mountain resort." Another one said, "From friends in Yokohama." The last one said, "From Mr. Itoh."

Eiko was deeply touched by each one who had sent flowers. "Mother, this Mr. Itoh is the head of the company where I work. The friends in Yokohama are the relatives of one of my coworkers, Satoh. The friends from the mountain resort are the friends of another coworker named Sayuri. That was so kind of them to send flowers."

Etsuko nodded. "Yes, it was. I also saw the money envelope you turned in from the Sakamotos, that nice family who lives near your apartment and who has befriended you. They gave a generous amount. I will prepare a proper thank-you gift for you to take back to them."

She stopped then and looked up, as if listening. "They are calling our name," she said with a sigh. "We are almost done, and soon we will return home with only our memories to comfort us in our grief."

Eiko followed behind her with a heavy heart, wondering if the pain would lessen with time.

A few more days passed, and it was time for Eiko to pack and return to Tokyo. Her two weeks in Sapporo had been hard, but she was glad she had come. Still, she was anxious to get back to her life in Tokyo and to her friends. Sayuri had phoned her several times, letting her know what was going on at work and asking how she was doing. Satoh had left a message on her home phone, which she was able to access, saying that he was thinking about her. The rest of his message was about how sad he felt that she took off for Hokkaido without telling him first. Eiko felt badly that she had run out of time before leaving Tokyo and that she didn't get around to making that call to Satoh.

On the flight back to Tokyo, Eiko thought more deeply about Satoh. She really should have told him personally about her papa's death, but she hadn't forgotten the way he had acted when he found out she was going with the church group to the mountain retreat. *He should have been happy for me. Or, he should have let me know sooner that he was going to ask his cousin if we could come for a visit. Who knows what I would have decided if I had known about Yokohama before my invitation to the mountains? Granted, Satoh and I hang out together sometimes, but nothing is written in stone.*

A few hours later, Eiko was sitting on her own sofa in her apartment when the doorbell rang. She frowned. *Who knows I am back already?* She opened the door to find Satoh standing there, flowers in hand. His face brightened the moment he saw her. "You are back! I was hoping I could see you today. I brought you flowers—just in case." He held them out to her.

She smiled and took them from him. "Arigatou for your thoughtfulness. Actually, I am glad you are here. I was going to call you and ask if we could get some dinner together."

Satoh's smile widened. "Sure. That would be great!"

"Let me put the flowers in a vase, and I will be right back," she said. "Wait here."

In less than five minutes, Eiko rejoined Satoh at the front door, her jacket and purse slung over her arm. The two then walked out into the crisp, early evening air.

"Do you want to get sushi for dinner?" Eiko asked.

"I had sushi for lunch. How about a coffee shop?"

"That is fine. There is one close by here. I will show you the way."

Satoh looked into Eiko's eyes before asking, "So how are you, Eiko chan? I know this time must be hard for you."

"I am okay." Hot tears stung her eyes, but she blinked them way. "It is really sad that I will not see my papa ever again."

Satoh sighed. "Yes. That is sad. Did his wake and funeral go well?"

She nodded. "Lots of people came to show their support. Even some family members we hardly ever see came."

"Nothing like a funeral to get all the family there." Satoh offered a comforting smile. "I am not family, but I wish I had been there. Since we went to Mrs. Itoh's wake together, it just seems sort of natural to be at another such service together."

Eiko did her best to return his smile. "Arigatou. That is kind of you, Satoh kun. I actually thought about our experience at Mrs. Itoh's wake, too, because no one knows where the soul is going in a Buddhist ceremony. My mother put coins in my papa's suit pocket to use on his journey. Yet the church people thought about Mrs. Itoh already at home in heaven with Jesus, her Savior. It really is about eternity, I think."

Satoh appeared confused. "What is?"

"Eternity," she repeated. "It should be on our hearts all the time. Where do we want to spend eternity?"

"I do not think we can choose, Eiko chan. I think it is chosen for us—a matter of fate."

Eiko shook her head. "I do not want to believe that. I want to believe what I learned at the mountain retreat about the Bible, that God gave us free will. He did not make us robots. He hoped we would choose Him—choose to be in a relationship with Him."

Satoh stopped walking and looked at her with such concern that she too stopped. "Is that what you have done?" he asked. "Have you chosen to be in a relationship with the Christian God?"

"Not yet," she admitted. "But knowing what happens to us when we die sure makes living our lives a lot less stressful. My friend had a Christian tell him that reading the Bible and praying helped him not to get stressed. Maybe that is what your cousin meant when he said he feels whole, now that he is a Christian."

They walked a few more steps and arrived at their destination. "Speaking of my cousin," Satoh said after they had been seated, "we are invited to visit him and his new wife soon, at their apartment. Is that something you still want to do?"

They gave the waitress their order and then continued with their conversation.

"Yes, definitely," Eiko answered. "I would like to get to know Aki and Yoko. How are they doing, now that the wedding is behind them?"

"They are extremely happy," Satoh answered, "though there was some drama on their wedding day, which I did not tell you about. Yoko, who was adopted by the pastor and his wife when she was a baby, has a biological sister. The sister showed up at the church, really drunk, saying she could not stay for the wedding because she was too much of a sinner to come into the church. While the pastor and his wife counseled with Yoko's sister in their home, which is connected to the church, my cousin and I went to buy some strong coffee and stomach medicine in hopes that would help her feel well enough to stay. Aki said that he and Yoko had prayed for months that her sister would come and be a part of their special day."

Eiko understood then. "So that is where you went after the church service."

Satoh nodded. "I was asked to be a support for Aki, as he supported his wife."

"How did it end?"

He smiled. "The sister stayed for the ceremony, sitting right next to the pastor's wife. My cousin said his in-laws are great examples of caring for people the way Jesus did."

Eiko smiled too, pleased at Satoh's words. "That paints a picture for Yoko's sister that Jesus is a friend of sinners. Sayuri, my friend from work, says that Jesus' grace—undeserved favor, she calls it—is for everyone. Everyone needs it, but not everyone chooses to receive it."

Satoh looked thoughtful. "Maybe some people are not looking for it because they do not know they need it. Other people just do not want any help, I guess."

Eiko nodded, as the waitress brought their orders. "But happy are those who choose to receive His grace," she said before they began to eat, remembering someone speaking those words at the retreat.

Satoh appeared ready to challenge her last statement, but instead he took a bite of food, as did she. They ate in relative silence, then stood up and took the bill to the counter to pay it.

"I have got this, Eiko chan."

"I invited you, Satoh kun. My mother sent me home with some money."

"Save it for later," Satoh suggested. "I am so happy you are home. Thanks for going out with me tonight."

"You are very welcome, Satoh kun," she replied as she smiled up at him.

The weeks went by quickly after that dinner. At work, things continued to get busier, as the company became even more successful when the god-shelf was removed. Many employees still worried that it would cause a decline because the gods would be angry. Instead, each wise saying, written in beautiful calligraphy and hanging on the newly painted wall, impressed a lot of people. A different saying appeared on the first day of each month. Sayuri told Eiko that the wise sayings about how to do business were from the book of Proverbs in the Bible.

Eiko was happy to work for Mr. Itoh, and the next time she saw him, she thanked him personally for the flowers he sent for her papa's funeral. She told him how much they meant to her, and he responded by telling her he was sorry she had lost her father.

In addition, Eiko's friendship with Sayuri blossomed, as they spent more time together. When Sayuri invited Eiko to be part of a college Bible study at her church on Thursday nights, Eiko readily accepted. She attended regularly and was pleased to be using the New Testament Bible she had received at Mrs. Itoh's wake.

Hope Tanner also kept in touch. She wrote that she was happy to hear that Eiko was attending Bible study. She encouraged Eiko to read the Bible on her own, to learn more about God and how much He loves her by sending Jesus to die in her place. Hope also taught Eiko how to pray, by just opening up her heart to talk to God about anything and everything. "He is always there, listening," Hope wrote. Eiko looked forward to her letters from Hope and often read them more than once.

Things with Satoh had been good, too. They spent time getting to know each other and enjoyed being together. They enjoyed a fun weekend with Satoh's cousin Aki and his wife, Yoko. The two couples went to a concert and afterward made dinner together. Eiko was able to ask them questions about their faith in Jesus and what it means to be a Christian. Although Satoh didn't ask any questions, he listened politely, and that encouraged Eiko.

At least once a week, Eiko and Satoh ate lunch at their favorite ramen place. Satoh continually teased her about eating Hokkaido ramen when she returned to Sapporo for her father's funeral.

The Sakamoto family started inviting Eiko over for dinner once a week. She appreciated their kindness and enjoyed being with them as much, or more, than she enjoyed her own family. In some ways, the Sakamotos reminded Eiko of her own family when they were younger, particularly when her father was still alive.

When Eiko returned to Tokyo after her papa's death, the Sakamoto family received a famous wood carving from Eiko's mother as a thank-you gift for their special support of her daughter. The carving of a Hokkaido bear, fishing for salmon, was now displayed proudly in their living room. Eiko saw it every time she entered their home, which somehow made their two families seem more closely connected.

Eiko's mother had not done well in the weeks that followed the funeral. Suffering from depression, she rarely left the house. Her brother stayed away as much as he could, coming home mostly to sleep. Their mother's main focus every day became taking care of the family cat.

Eiko found herself praying for her mother and brother, asking church friends to pray for them as well. Eiko continued to call home several times a week. Sometimes her mother picked up the phone; at other times, she let it ring. During the first week of December, Eiko called and waited for her mother to pick up. Thankfully, this time, she did. But the moment Eiko heard her mother speak, she was stunned at how much older she sounded.

As Eiko paused, pondering the obvious change in her mother's voice, Etsuko asked, "Are you okay, Eiko?"

"Me? Yes. I am. But how are you, Mother? Are you feeling any better?"

After a brief hesitation, she answered, "About the same."

"Do you know what day this is?" Eiko asked, hoping to get her mother's mind on something more positive.

"No, I do not. Is it a holiday that I missed?"

"No, but it is the first day of December. That means the holidays are coming soon."

The older woman sighed loudly. "I suppose so."

"Mom, remember how Papa loved getting the family together on December twenty-third, how he loved to give Christmas gifts to each of us?" Even as she spoke the words, she realized she had called her mother "mom," something she seldom did, preferring instead to use the more formal title of "mother." Was it possible she was feeling even closer to Etsuko, now that they shared such a painful loss?

Her mother's answer was abrupt, driving out some of Eiko's feelings of closeness with her. "This year we cannot celebrate, Eiko. It is not right. Your father has only been gone a few weeks. It is not proper."

It was Eiko's turn to sigh. "People in Japan are free to do what they want these days, Mother. Not every tradition has to be kept perfectly, as in the olden days."

"We Japanese need tradition. It has kept us going for thousands of years."

"All right, so what about New Year's? Are you going to celebrate those three days?"

"I will not be sending out any New Year's postcards, but I do want your brother to take me to the temple to get the New Year blessing. Everyone should know how badly we need it."

Eiko paused at the sudden thought that popped into her mind, then decided to go ahead. "Mother, I want to come home for a visit. Our company is closing down during the New Year's holidays. Every employee will get five days off. Our boss is very generous. He said he wants everyone to spend time with their families while they can. I am going to ask him if I can have two weeks off without pay. Maybe my being home will help you feel better."

"That's nice, dear. Yes, we will expect you to come. The cat will be especially happy to see you. I need to let Kiku outside now, so I will talk to you again soon."

When the conversation had ended and the two women had hung up, Eiko's heart was heavy with worry. She grabbed her Bible and opened it, letting the pages fall as they would. Looking down at the opened pages, she read 1 Peter 5:7: "Give all your worries to him, because he cares about you." She closed her eyes and prayed aloud. "Lord, I ask You to help my mother be more positive about living life without Papa. Help her with her grief during the difficult holiday period. Help her to know that You exist and that You are the only *good* God. There is no other. Amen."

Another two weeks passed before the weekend of the children's Christmas party at church finally arrived. On Saturday afternoon, Eiko and Sayuri came out of the store, carrying several bags.

Eiko was pleased with their purchases. "We got a great bargain on the hot chocolate and cookies."

Sayuri nodded. "I think the Lord helped us to stay under budget. I do not think I have seen these items on sale before."

"The party is going to be fun for the kids. I wonder how the other teams are doing with their preparations." Eiko smiled. "I am glad we could be the team responsible for the snacks. I sure hope lots of children come."

"Hopefully, many kids from the neighborhood will show up. The advertisement team passed out a hundred invitations, door-to-door, last week."

When they got back to the church, they ran into friends their age, whom Eiko had met at the singles' retreat and had gotten to know at the Bible studies. It was their group that was helping put on the party on Sunday afternoon.

Everyone pitched in to help clean and decorate the party room, which had tile flooring, except for a small tatami area for sitting. A tiny kitchen was located in the far corner of the room. Nearby stood a four-foot artificial Christmas tree, decorated with angels the children had made the previous Sunday. Below the tree was a small wooden crate, with a doll representing the baby Jesus, resting comfortably on the straw, which had been placed inside. On the wall above hung a banner that read " 'Glory to God in the highest heaven, and peace on earth to those with whom he is pleased!' (Luke 2:14, GNB)."

The children will love this, Eiko thought, as they finished displaying some Christmas wreaths and nativity scenes. Then it was time to get going.

Eiko said goodbye to the other workers, as she picked up her bag and headed toward the door. "Sorry," she explained, "but I need to be at my neighbor's house for dinner. See you tomorrow!"

"Thanks for your help," several people called out. "See you tomorrow!"

Eiko hurried but still arrived at the Sakamotos' house five minutes late.

"I am sorry to be late and to cause you to wait dinner on me," she said when Mrs. Sakamoto opened the door.

"Not a problem," the woman answered, ushering her guest inside and toward the kitchen. "I am still cooking, and Mr. Sakamoto went out on an errand with one of the boys. They will be back shortly. Would you like to help me cut some fruit?"

Eiko was eager to help. "Sure. What do you need me to prepare?"

"My neighbor gave me some persimmons. Would you slice them and put them on this plate? We will have them after dinner."

As Eiko sliced the fruit, Mr. Sakamoto and his sons, Ichirou and Daisuke, arrived and greeted Eiko warmly.

"Everyone wash up for dinner. It is ready," Mrs. Sakamoto said.

In a matter of minutes, they had all sat down at the dining room table and said Itadakimasu in unison. As they began to pass around the bowls and plates of food, Mrs. Sakamoto said, "Eiko chan, be sure and get some pickles. I made them myself."

"They really taste good," Ichirou, the older son, told Eiko. "I have been eating them for fifteen years." He grinned, looking very much like his father when his dark eyes twinkled. "That is why I am so blessed."

"You really ate them when you were a baby?" Daisuke asked in obvious disbelief.

Eiko smiled and nodded. "I will definitely eat some. Everything looks so delicious! I appreciate your invitation tonight."

Mr. Sakamoto smiled. "We are happy to share with you," he said, as he sipped his miso soup. "How are things going with you?"

"Okay. This afternoon I helped my friends get ready for a children's Christmas party at church. I think the kids are going to have a great time."

Mr. Sakamoto's face lit up. "Do you have *mikans* to pass out to all the kids?"

"No, we don't. We just have cookies and hot chocolate to drink."

"Why don't I pick up a box of them at the wholesalers' market early tomorrow morning? I would like to donate a box. I can deliver them to the church before the party."

Eiko smiled, her heart warmed by the man's generosity. She knew how much the children would enjoy the small, easy-to-peel citrus fruit. "Arigatou gozaimasu! That is really sweet of you. I know the children will be pleased."

"I remember going to a children's party at church when I was young," Mr. Sakamoto said. "It made a big impression on me. This is a way I can give back."

"Do you go to that church often?" Mrs. Sakamoto asked Eiko, an edge of concern in her voice.

"Lately I have been going often, yes, ever since the singles' retreat. The people are really nice. I found out I have more in common with them than I thought." She used her chopsticks to pick up a bite of tuna.

The conversation changed then to what the Sakamoto boys had been up to the last few weeks at school and in their school clubs. Later, As Eiko left for the evening, Mrs. Sakamoto handed her a bag of some of the leftover persimmons. Eiko loved their sweet taste and was happy to take some with her.

Once home, Eiko called her mother to see how she was doing.

"Hi, Mother. It's Eiko. How was your Saturday? Was it a good day?"

Etsuko was a bit more talkative than she had been lately, but Eiko could still hear the deep sadness in her voice. "Your uncle's best friend from college came by the house today. He and his wife live in southern Japan, but they are visiting Sapporo for two weeks. He brought a package that he said he wanted you to have, something that belonged to your father when he was younger. I told him you are coming home on Christmas Eve, and you can get it then. He said that would be fine. I have put it in your bedroom, dear, for when you get here."

Eiko's curiosity was already tempting her to ask her mother to open it and tell her what it was, but she resisted. Better to wait and open it personally when she got there. "Arigatou, Mom. I cannot imagine what it is, but it will be nice to have something that belonged to Papa." She realized she had just said "mom" again, rather than "mother," but this time it seemed more natural.

They spoke a few more minutes until Eiko said, "Well, I have a busy day tomorrow at church and need to get my rest, so I had better hang up now."

Her mother paused briefly before speaking. "Are you still going to that church? Why do you go? Don't you have more important things to do on Sundays?"

"Mother, it makes me happy to go. The people are like family to me."

Now the hurt was evident in her mother's voice. "What about your real family?"

"You are important to me, of course, Mother. That is why I will be home with you for the holidays."

"Okay, then," Etsuko said, though Eiko could tell her mother really wasn't okay with her church attendance.

"See you in five more days.," Eiko said. "And take care ... Mom."

"Okay, dear," Etsuko said, as her voice trailed off.

Eiko hung up the phone. She had been worrying about her mother's health since Papa's funeral. Now her mother was showing continued signs that life no longer held any meaning for her. Eiko knew what she must do the next day. She would ask her church friends to pray specifically that her mother would be able to relax and enjoy the holidays, despite her great loss.

Eiko woke up on Sunday morning with great excitement, and before long she was on her way to church. Today the children's Christmas party would take place after the morning worship service. She couldn't wait to see the children's happy faces when they saw all the decorations and treats.

As she entered the church, several people greeted her warmly.

"Eiko san, ohayou gozaimasu," an older lady called out to her. "We met your friend this morning. He left about forty minutes ago, but he left a box of mikans for the children's party."

Eiko recognized the woman as the one who prepared the *ikebana*, flower arrangement, for the church each week.

"That would have been Mr. Sakamoto," Eiko explained. "He asked me yesterday if we had some for the party. When I told him we did not, he said he was going to the wholesale market early this morning and would bring us some."

The woman seemed quite pleased. "What a lovely gesture! Be sure and thank him for us, please. It is not very often that we see such kindness from a stranger."

"I will," Eiko promised. "I will tell him today on my way home."

Eiko then found a place to sit by her friends, as the service was about to start. The pianist began to play, and Christmas carols soon filled the room. The pastor, Maki *sensei*, followed with a message about the real meaning of Christmas, the birth of God's only Son, Jesus. A beautiful Japanese calligraphy, taken from Matthew 1:23, hung at the front of the room, capturing the heart of the moment: "Immanuel, God is with us."

"God knew we needed a Savior," the pastor said, "so He sent His one and only Son, Jesus, into the world as a newborn baby. Jesus lived his entire life doing the will of God, His Father. Jesus showed us how much God loved us, how far Almighty God would go to have relationship with us. Jesus willingly died on the Cross in our place, taking our sin and punishment upon Himself, even though He lived a perfect life. God then accepted his Son's death as the once-for-all payment necessary for our sin of unbelief. God raised Jesus from the dead after three days, and now we, too, have conquered death through Him. Those who trust in Jesus, asking Him to be their personal Savior and Lord, are completely forgiven and invited to live forever with Him in heaven after we die. This is what God desires for all the people He lovingly created."

I want Jesus to be my Savior and Lord, Eiko whispered in her heart, as it began stirring. *I want to experience that kind of love from a God who desires to spend eternity with me.* Tears began to trickle from Eiko's eyes, though she tried to stop them. Hanako, a friend she had met at the singles retreat and who now sat next to her, placed her hand on Eiko's shoulder and began to pray silently for her.

CHAPTER TEN

As Hanako prayed for Eiko, the pastor, asked for anyone needing prayer to come to the front of the church. Eiko quickly stepped out of her row and walked toward the front. She came face-to-face with Maki sensei and told him she was ready to trust Jesus as her Savior. The pastor smiled and nodded, then laid a hand on her shoulder and began to pray, asking her to repeat after him that she needed forgiveness, she believed in Jesus as the Son of God, and she wanted to receive Him as her Savior and Lord. After praying together, the pastor spoke to her briefly and then moved on to pray for someone else, as Eiko sat down on the front row, her heart soaring with joy she knew she couldn't begin to express.

After the service, the pastor told the church that Eiko san and an older man, Nagai san, had made decisions to trust in Christ and had agreed to be baptized at the Christmas Eve service on Thursday afternoon at 4:30. After the pastor's final prayer, Eiko received kind words and a few hugs from people in the church. A good number said they would be at the Christmas Eve service to see her baptized.

"I am so happy for you!" said Wada, the singles' director, who first met Eiko at the retreat in the mountains.

"Thank you, Wada san. The Lord has been speaking to my heart ever since the retreat. Today, I did not want to fight it any longer. I am ready to make a commitment to Jesus. I have experienced His love and have seen Him change my heart-attitude and desires. I am really happy, so happy because of Jesus. Even though my family situation is rough right now, and I do not have any clue what will happen in the future, I am at peace."

Wada nodded. "Yes. He is our peace. I love what His Word says about that. It says that His peace is a peace the world cannot understand—only those who have come to know Him personally as Lord and Savior. That is the peace you are experiencing now."

Eiko nodded, her heart full to overflowing with joy.

After a special lunch, prepared by the women of the church, things were quickly transitioned to welcome the children to their Christmas party. The colorful decorations the singles had put up the day before, along with the Christmas treats, caught the eyes of the children as soon as they came in.

"Eiko," a young boy whispered, after he motioned for her to lean down to hear him, "there is someone outside named Satoh, asking about you."

Pleasantly surprised, Eiko exclaimed, "Oh, please, tell him where I am, and ask him to come in."

When Satoh walked through the doorway a few moments later, their eyes met, and both smiled. "Uh, sorry, Eiko chan," he said as he approached. "I hope you do not mind. You told me about the party, so I came to help ... if it is okay."

"Satoh kun, yes, of course. Right now we are blowing up some balloons for a race. Can you help?"

"That happens to be one of my special skills," Satoh said, with what appeared to be a relieved grin.

They grabbed the green and red balloons and began trying to inflate them, but it proved a little more difficult than they thought. As they kept trying, the children cheered them on. "Do not give up!" they shouted. "You can do it!"

As soon as a few of the balloons were successfully filled, the children began tossing them up in the air, even as the helpers tried to encourage them to put them back on the table.

One of the church workers, who was in charge of the game, called out in her pleasant but firm voice, "Okay. I need all the kids to line up in three rows, so let us count off and divide into groups. There are thirty children, so there should be ten in each of the three rows."

The kids quickly got into their groups, ready to start. Two children from each row had to partner together to get their balloon to the other side of the room and back. The balloon was placed in between them, as they stood back to back with their arms locked together. One child had to walk backwards, and on the return trip the other child walked backwards. Walking in harmony was the goal. Giggles and gasps filled the room each time a pair fell down and had to start again.

After the winners of the game were given a prize, the children were asked to stand around the tables that had already been prepared. One of the workers passed out hand wipes for everyone to clean their hands, while another gave the instructions.

"Everyone has five sugar cookies in these cute take-out boxes," she explained. "They are to take home to your families today. First, you need to put some frosting on your cookies with a plastic knife. Then decorate them, using the star decorations, the sprinkles, or the other goodies at your table."

"Can we eat them?" a small girl asked.

The worker smiled. "Not these. We have something special prepared for you to eat in just a little while. Please remember—do not eat the decorations, so there will be enough for everyone to use. Let us get started, okay? Several church friends are standing around to help you. If you need help, just raise your hand and someone will come."

There was a brief moment of silence, as the children grabbed plastic knives to spread the frosting on each cookie. A few minutes later, several of the children were already happily decorating with sprinkles and other goodies. Eiko saw an older boy who hadn't started yet, and she motioned Satoh to go with her to help him.

"I do not have a family to give these to," the boy explained. "It is only my mother and me, and she is too ill to eat cookies."

"Well, maybe you could give the cookies to a family friend," Satoh suggested.

The boy shrugged. "Maybe."

With Satoh's kind encouragement, the older boy decorated his cookies, and Eiko's heart warmed at her friend's behavior toward the boy.

As the children finished, they were told to carefully place their cookies back in the small take-out box. They then wrote their names on the top of the box so they could claim them later.

"Everyone come sit down on the tatami floor," the pastor called out. When they had done so, he said a few words of introduction to the children, and then turned on a children's animated Bible DVD of the first Christmas.

Eiko noticed that Satoh watched the DVD with apparent interest. She guessed he was hearing this Bible story for the first time. She, herself, had only read it in her own Bible a few weeks ago. Eiko looked forward to talking to Satoh about it after the party. Besides, she also had something to tell him that she thought he should know right away.

The children listened well until the end. Then the pastor asked, "Would someone like to pray and thank God for the gift of His only Son, Jesus, who came into this world to show us how much God loves us?"

The boy who talked to Satoh earlier volunteered. "Thank You, God, that You gave us the best gift of all...Jesus. Thank You for sharing Him with us so we could hear about Your love and be saved. Amen."

Two young women came out of the kitchen then, carefully carrying a decorated Christmas cake with candles all aglow. Someone dimmed the room lights, as a man began singing softly and with reverence, "Happy birthday to You, Happy Birthday to You, Happy birthday, dear Jesus, Happy birthday to You!"[iii]

The children clapped as the lights came back on. Everyone received a piece of cake, along with a mikan, some cookies, and hot chocolate. Satoh helped Eiko and the other workers make sure all the children got served. When the parents arrived, the children were handed their personally decorated cookies for their families, and also a small book of the Christmas story. The party had come to an end, and everyone involved was happy with the results.

"That was fun!" Satoh said, as he and Eiko left the church together after helping to clean up.

"Yes. I loved helping," Eiko agreed. "It was nice to see the kids so happy and excited."

"It would have been nice to have experienced this when I was a kid. No one I knew ever went to church," Satoh admitted.

---

iii Public Domain.

Eiko nodded. "When I was in elementary school, I had a friend in my neighborhood who went to church. She became a Christian, and I remember hearing her talk about God's love. I could tell God meant a lot to her. Whenever she had problems, she would always pray to Him. Now I can totally understand, but back then I thought it was strange."

"Totally understand?" Satoh looked puzzled. "What does that mean?"

"Actually, Satoh, there is something I need to tell you." She shot up a silent prayer, took a deep breath, and went on. "Today, after Maki sensei's message, I made a decision to follow Christ. I asked God to forgive me for my self-centeredness and invited His only Son, Jesus, into my heart to be my Savior and Lord."

The look of confusion on Satoh's face quickly changed to unbelief. "You did what? Why? You have only been going to church a little while. You cannot know enough yet. Did they pressure you?"

"Satoh kun, you were with the church people at the party today. Do you really think they pushed me into making a decision?"

"Well, no... not really," he admitted. "But it does not make any sense."

"It only makes sense to those who have faith to believe. I asked God to show me if He was real, and He did. I know He is real. I know Jesus died to take the punishment that was meant for me. I know He rose again and now offers abundant life to all who trust in His name. I know I am saved. I have received a brand new heart that wants to please Jesus. The joy I have is real, Satoh kun."

"But..." Satoh paused, as if unsure what to say next. At last, he continued. "What happens tomorrow? Will that joy still be there?"

"I know Jesus will never leave me. He will always be with me. That is where my joy each day will come from—His promise."

Satoh stopped walking and sighed. "My cousin and his wife are Christians, and now you, too. This is crazy!"

"Maybe God is showing you that it is not crazy at all. People you know and love are accepting God's love and offer of salvation. Maybe that means God wants to show you the same love, up close and personal, through us."

A flicker of anger crossed Satoh's face, and he shook his head. "That will be the day. I am not interested, Eiko chan. I am sorry if that makes me bad, but I do not know what else to say."

Eiko wasn't sure how to respond. She opened her mouth to speak, but Satoh spoke first.

I need to be on my way somewhere," Satoh announced. "Catch you later, Eiko."

Off he went, leaving her to walk the rest of the way to the train station by herself. Even though she was sad about Satoh's reaction, the love of God was overflowing like a spring inside of her, bringing comfort. She would pray for Satoh to know God's love for him, as she did.

On the way home, Eiko decided to visit the Sakamotos. The store was already closed for the day, so she wasn't able to use the stairway inside their market, which led upstairs to their home. Instead, she opened a side door on the street, which offered another staircase up to their home.

"It is Eiko," she called, as she knocked on the door.

Within moments, Mrs. Sakamoto had opened the door. "Come in, please," she said. "What a nice surprise! How are you today?"

"Great," she said as she stepped inside. "I wanted to thank you for the mikans for the children's party at church."

The woman appeared puzzled. "Mikans for the children's party at church? Oh, that Papa! I completely forgot he was going to do that. Just a minute. I will go get him. I think he fell asleep watching TV."

"Please don't disturb him," she protested. "I can see him another time."

But Mrs. Sakamoto had already called out to her husband, as she left the room. "Husband, come on out here. Eiko chan wants to talk with you."

In a few moments, Mr. Sakamoto joined them, though his eyelids still looked heavy. "Oh, Eiko chan! It is nice to see you."

"I am so sorry I interfered with your rest time, Mr. Sakamoto. I came by to thank you for the mikans. The children loved them. They were really delicious. It was so kind of you to do that."

He smiled. "I was happy to do it, Eiko chan. Memories of my visits to church still warm my heart."

Placing four small take-out boxes on the kitchen table, she said, "I brought you some sugar cookies from the party. I thought you and your family might enjoy them."

Mrs. Sakamoto smiled. "Arigatou, Eiko chan."

"I also came by to tell you about something special that happened today, something I especially wanted you to know about." A mixture of nerves and excitement fluttered in her stomach. "I became a Christian today. I made the decision to trust in Christ as my Savior and Lord."

"Good for you!" Mr. Sakamoto exclaimed, his face beaming with pleasure.

Mrs. Sakamoto did not look so pleased. "What will your poor mother say? Do you think she is strong enough right now to experience another big shock in the family?"

Mr. Sakamoto frowned. "Wife, be quiet. Do not say those troublesome things to Eiko chan. Can you not see how happy she is? She is glowing from the inside out!"

Eiko blushed and nodded. "It has been a wonderful day, one I will never forget. I am extremely happy. I look forward to learning more about God and His love for me each new day. By the way, I am getting baptized this Thursday, on Christmas Eve, at four-thirty at our church. I would love it if you would come."

"Is that not the day you fly home to spend the holidays with your mother?" Mrs. Sakamoto asked.

Eiko nodded. "Yes, it is. But I will still be able to catch the last flight to Sapporo that night."

"Would it not be better to wait until you get back from the holidays?" It did not appear that Mrs. Sakamoto would let go of the topic easily. "What is the rush to get baptized?"

"There is no rush," Eiko explained. "I am just eager to tell others what He has done for me."

Mr. Sakamoto still smiled. "I would love to come, Eiko chan. You can count on me being there."

"That means a lot to me. Arigatou gozaimasu," Eiko said, though she was disappointed that it appeared Mrs. Sakamoto wouldn't be coming with her husband. "Well, I had better get going. It is time for me to head home and get some things done."

Mr. Sakamoto stood at the door as she left. "See you on Thursday, Eiko chan."

"Yes," she said with a smile. "See you then!"

Monday morning dawned without a cloud in the sky. Looking up at nihonbare, Eiko decided it matched the condition of her heart. Climbing the last few steps up to her office building, she rejoiced, knowing she had a personal relationship with Creator God who made the brilliant blue sky.

"Ohayou gozaimasu, Eiko san," Sayuri said, as Eiko got off the elevator. They walked together to Eiko's desk. "I am sorry I was not at church yesterday, but my family had an emergency. When I called Pastor last night, he told me you had some good news to share with me."

"Life-changing news," Eiko replied with a grin. "Want to have lunch together?"

"Yes. How about the park?"

"It is a beautiful day to have lunch in the park. Yes. I will meet you in the lobby, and we can walk there together."

The morning flew by, and before Eiko realized it, it was lunchtime. She and Sayuri walked to the park together, then sat down on a bench. As each one opened her obentou and started to eat, Eiko shared with Sayuri the details of what had happened the previous day. They then talked about her decision to be baptized on Thursday night, the children's party, and even Satoh's reaction to Eiko's decision to become a Christian. Sayuri's joyous response was a great encouragement to Eiko.

As they spoke, Eiko realized how blessed she was to have at least one other Christian at her workplace. Sayuri was surely a gift from God. *Thank You, Lord*, she prayed silently.

The rest of the day went quickly, and Eiko was on her way to the train station, headed for home, when Satoh caught up with her. "Eiko chan, will you have lunch with me tomorrow at the ramen shop, please?" Concern showed in his eyes as he spoke. "I am really sorry about yesterday."

"Sure, Satoh kun. Tomorrow for lunch is fine." She smiled. "I would like that very much."

The words of Satoh's apology echoed in her heart, even after she was home. Before going to bed, she poured out her heart in prayer. "Lord, I do not know what to do to help Satoh. Please help me tomorrow as we meet together."

The next day, Satoh was quiet as they walked to the ramen shop together. After they were seated and had ordered their noodles, Satoh looked into her eyes and began to speak.

"Eiko chan, I admit there might be something to this God thing you have going for you. I want you to know that I will keep an open mind. Ever since I sat by you at Mrs. Itoh's wake, I have enjoyed being with you in church. Also, the shared experience we had together at my cousin's church when he got married was fun. And you already know how much I enjoyed helping out at the children's party. So I am open to going to church with you sometimes. But I am just telling you—I am not perfect, and I am not planning on trying to be."

Eiko's answer was soft but clear. "Everyone is imperfect, Satoh. Only Jesus is perfect and good. When we trust in Jesus as Savior and Lord, He lives inside us. When Holy God looks at us, He does not see our imperfections. He only sees His perfect Son, living in us, and He is pleased. That is His amazing love."

Satoh nodded. "It sounds amazing, but it also sounds too good to be true."

Ignoring his remark, Eiko asked Satoh to come to her baptism. "How about it? You have been to a wake and a wedding in a church; how about a Christmas Eve service and a baptism?"

"The other times we went together," Satoh answered, his words hinting at uncertainty, "but this time I will be sitting alone."

She put her hand on his arm. "I would really like for you to be there."

He sighed. "Okay. I will be there."

"Wonderful!" Eiko exclaimed, thrilled to know that not only Mr. Sakamoto would be at church to see her baptized, but Satoh as well.

After working all day Tuesday, Eiko decided to relax at home that evening. She was happy that Wednesday was a day off for everyone because of the national holiday, celebrating the Emperor's birthday. That gave her plenty of time to prepare for her trip to Sapporo, by doing laundry and other chores. Eiko didn't hear anything from Satoh, but she wasn't worried. She counted on seeing him and Mr. Sakamoto at the baptism the next day.

Early Thursday morning, Eiko finished doing some Christmas shopping and put the last few items in her travel bag. After a quick lunch of leftovers, she sat down with her Bible for a quiet time. After reading for a while, she closed with a prayer: "Lord, arigatou for all that You are doing in my life. I am glad that I am Your child. Thank You for being real to me, for giving me friends who could teach me about You. Help me to do that for others."

Eiko changed into some black slacks and a red sweater before grabbing a towel and a pair of beige slacks and a beige shirt, which she would wear under a white robe when she was baptized. A church friend had offered to pick her up in a car because she also had to take her bag with her for the airport. She had gratefully accepted.

The phone rang then, and Eiko answered.

"Hello, Eiko. This is Hope Tanner."

"Hope, it is so good to hear from you! How are you? Are you returning to America today?"

"Yes, I am. I just arrived in Tokyo from Sapporo. I have a few hours before my flight to America this evening. Do you have time to meet me?"

Eiko sighed, disappointed. "I am so sorry, but my schedule will not allow it. I am getting baptized in just a little while, at my church's Christmas Eve service."

"Eiko, that's wonderful! I'm so happy for you! Jesus is your faithful Shepherd and Friend. Every day with Him is special."

Eiko nodded, though she knew Hope couldn't see her. "You are so right. Thank you for the encouragement. I would like to learn more about what God is doing in your life. Let us keep in touch. That is awesome that you spent two years of your life in Sapporo."

"I had a wonderful time, even though there were some real challenges." She hesitated before saying, "By the way, where is your church, and what time is the baptism? I might be able to make it."

Eiko caught her breath. "Really? You will not be late for your plane?"

"No. I think it will be all right. I might not be able to stay for the whole service, but hopefully I can be there for your baptism."

Thrilled at yet another friend being there to watch her baptized, Eiko gave Hope the name and location of the church. "I think the baptism will be the first thing on the program," Eiko said. "The service starts at four-thirty."

"Okay. Thanks. I hope to see you there!"

Eiko grabbed her things and locked the apartment door, her ride waiting downstairs. She was pleasantly surprised that God had apparently arranged for Hope to be at her baptism. They had gotten to know one another primarily by phone, as well as the few times they had met face-to-face. Throughout that time, Hope had become a trusted friend to Eiko.

The church brimmed with excitement as people walked in. Nagai san, the elderly man who was also being baptized, was already there. Several people were happily setting things up, making sure everything was in place before the guests arrived.

Thirty minutes before the service started, every seat seemed taken, except for the first row, which was saved for those being baptized and others who had a part in the program. A few men headed to the room where the children's party had taken place. They brought back some folding chairs, which they placed in the back and along the side walls of the worship center to handle the overflow crowd.

It was time. The pianist started playing, as the soloist stood to sing "O Holy Night." The beautiful vibrato of the soprano voice filled the room with thoughts of that beautiful starlit night in Bethlehem. As the song ended, Maki sensei came out in a white robe and stood in a special enclosed space, known as a baptismal, behind the pulpit, which held waist-deep water.

"Tonight we celebrate that holy night about two thousand years ago," he said, "when God's promise of sending the Messiah, the Savior of the world, came to pass. On that night, shepherds worshiped the newborn baby, wrapped in swaddling clothes and lying in a lowly place, where animals were kept. As God's glory shone around them, the shepherds knelt in worship and awe. They knew it was no ordinary birth and no ordinary baby. It was God's perfect Son, who had left heaven to come to earth as Immanuel, God-with-us. Tonight we are about to see Eiko san and Nagai san baptized because they want to testify that they, too, are followers of Jesus Christ, God's Son."

He reached out his hand to Eiko, who took it as she stepped down into the water. He waited then, until she stood next to him. "Eiko san, have you trusted in Jesus as your Savior and Lord?"

"Yes, I have."

"Please share your faith testimony."

She looked out at the crowd, her heart swelling with joy, particularly when she caught sight of Mr. Sakamoto and Satoh, as well as Hope and Sayuri and many of her other church friends. "Up until four months ago," she began, "I did not really know the truth that God loves me and has a plan for me. I am so grateful that He used the circumstances and people in my life to reveal Himself, and also His love for me, in clear, undeniable ways. Last Sunday, at this church, I could not resist His love any longer. I knew I was ready to commit to be His follower for the rest of my life. I repented of my unbelief and trusted in His Son, Jesus Christ, as my Savior and Lord."

When she finished, the pastor spoke again. "Being immersed in the water shows the picture that we have been buried with Him in death, and being raised up out of the water symbolizes our new life in Christ. Eiko san, in the name of the Father, Son, and Holy Spirit, I baptize you, my sister in the Lord." Eiko was gently laid back in the water and raised up again by holding onto the pastor's arm. She came up dripping wet, with a huge smile on her face. As she stepped out of the baptismal, Nagai san entered. Eiko wrapped herself in a towel and waited in the wings, where she could see and hear the elderly man's baptism.

"As you can see," he said, after the pastor had asked him to share his testimony, "I am in the winter of my life. I do not know how many years I have left. I have had many opportunities since childhood to learn about God, but I chose to do other things. Now I have such joy in my heart, since I prayed and professed my faith in God, apologizing to Him for my self-centeredness. I am envious of Eiko san because she has more years to walk with Jesus on this earth than I do. But I am extremely grateful to experience His love every moment of each day."

Nagai san took hold of the pastor's arm and was gently leaned back in the water. Eiko heard the pastor's words, "I baptize you, my brother in Christ, in the name of the Father, the Son, and the Holy Spirit." Nagai san stepped out of the water, and they each headed back to their separate changing rooms.

Eiko hurried because she didn't want to miss the rest of the service. When she re-entered the sanctuary, she quietly made her way to the front pew, where she'd been instructed to sit. Nagai was already there, and they exchanged joyful smiles.

The remainder of the worship time was spent singing Christmas carols, listening to the Bible being read, and concluding with a special candlelight time, while everyone joined together in singing "Silent Night." The last prayer was said, and the candles were extinguished. After the final amen, the lights came back on, and Eiko san and Nagai san were greeted by well-wishers.

Hope was among the first to greet Eiko. "It was a beautiful baptism. I'm so glad I could make it, but I need to leave now, so I won't be late for my flight. I'll keep in touch with you, and I'll be praying for you, as you spend time with your family in Sapporo over the holidays." She hugged Eiko and left before Eiko could say anything more than "thank you."

Others stood around Eiko, rejoicing with her and wishing her well. Some thanked her for her testimony. She glanced over at Nagai san, who was talking with a man who looked familiar. Briefly staring in that direction, she realized it was Mr. Sakamoto. *How wonderful!*

She looked around for Satoh, but couldn't find him in the crowd. Some people were beginning to leave, though, and soon it would be easier to spot him.

Sayuri approached then and handed her a little box. "This is a small gift to celebrate your baptism." She smiled. "It is only a framed photo of the meadow at the mountain retreat, but my real gift will be to paint the same scene for you in watercolors."

Eiko felt her eyes open wide. "How kind of you, Sayuri! I know what a talented painter you are. I will call you from Sapporo while I am away, so we can talk more."

Sayuri nodded. "That would be nice, but do not worry if you are too busy. By the way, Mr. Itoh was here tonight. He was sitting in the back of the church. He comes occasionally since his wife died."

Eiko was pleased. "I should pray for him to find God's love, too. He is a kind and generous man."

Sayuri nodded. "Mrs. Itoh prayed for him consistently while she was alive. She was hoping for him to love the same Christ she loved. She believed it would definitely happen someday—in God's perfect timing."

As Eiko glanced at her watch, she thought about what a wonderful lady Mrs. Itoh was and how much her husband must miss her. Her heart squeezed, as she thought of her own loss, then pulled her thoughts back to the moment. "Well, I guess I need to be on my way," she said to Sayuri and a few others who remained. "See you all again in the New Year!"

They called out words of blessing to her, as she hurried toward the exit. She nearly bumped into Satoh as she stepped outside.

"Oh," she cried. "Satoh kun! I could not find you in the crowd, but I was hoping you were here and would come and talk to me afterward."

"I planned to," he said, his shoulders drooping, "but I was uncomfortable with all those people gathered around you." He ventured a slight smile. "I am glad we ran into one another out here."

"Satoh kun, I am so glad you came. It means a lot to me."

"I would not have missed it," he said, his hands stuck in his jacket pockets.

"I need to hurry to the airport, Satoh," she said. "Maybe we can talk by phone later."

"Is it okay if I go to the airport with you? I can carry your bag."

She smiled. "That would be nice. I got a ride from my house to the church, but I was just going to take a train to the monorail, and then on to the airport. It would be good to have company."

Satoh took her bag and walked quickly down the street, with Eiko at his side. They rode the train together, then switched to the monorail. The train and monorail were both very crowded that evening because it was Christmas Eve. With the crush of people, Satoh and Eiko weren't able to talk much.

Finally, they reached the airport and made it to the check-in counter. After getting her boarding pass, Eiko walked towards Satoh and told him she had thirty minutes before she needed to go to her gate.

"Would you like something to drink?" Satoh asked. "Maybe a snack?"

"I am a little hungry," she admitted. "There is a place right over there that sells food."

Satoh asked what she wanted, then he went to the counter to make the purchase. He returned with their hot drinks and a sandwich. As they enjoyed their snack, Satoh pulled a small flat box out of his coat pocket.

"Eiko chan, this is a Christmas present for you. Please open it."

Eiko's heart leaped, as she said, "Satoh kun, I have something for you, too. It is in my bag. I planned to give it to you at church. Here, let me get it." She opened her bag and pulled out a small, soft package. "Here it is. You open yours first, and then I will open mine."

Satoh opened his gift and discovered a fashionable muffler that Eiko thought he might like. He wrapped it around his neck right away, as he thanked her.

Then Eiko opened her present and was surprised to see a beautiful sterling necklace with a heart charm. "Satoh kun, it is beautiful! I think you spent too much money on me."

"Eiko, I know I do not talk about my feelings," he mumbled, obviously self-conscious, "but I want this necklace to carry a message from me to you. I want to give you my heart. I feel happier with you than with anyone else I know."

Tears threatened her eyes, but she refused to allow them to stay. "Satoh kun, I am thankful that you are in my life, but my heart belongs to Jesus now. Can you give me some time? I need to pray about decisions that will affect my life, to see if it is what He wants for me. I promise to pray about our relationship."

Satoh nodded, looking only slightly dejected. "Okay, but just until the holidays are over. After that, I want to see you wear it."

Eiko reached out and grabbed Satoh's hand. "Thank you for understanding. I know God has a good plan for your life, too. He will show us what we should do. I trust His timing."

Satoh's face softened. "I know if we end up together, that means I will be spending lots of time in church."

Eiko grinned. "I think you are right. Some of that time might even be doing more children's programs."

"That would be okay with me," he admitted.

Eiko glanced at her watch again. "Oh, it is time for me to go. Thank you for coming with me to the airport and carrying my bag. That was so thoughtful."

He smiled. "Let me know when your return flight gets in, and I will be here to meet you."

She smiled again, pleased by his thoughtfulness. "Okay. I will."

"See you when you get back," he said, his voice husky.

Eiko turned and headed toward her gate. The passengers were already lining up and getting ready to board. She fell into line and was soon settling in to a window seat.

Eiko looked out the window, as the pilot waited for the control tower to give the okay to take off. Her thoughts turned to her family in Sapporo. She wondered how she would be able to help her mother, suffering with depression, and how her brother was handling the added pressure. Then she remembered the package her papa's friend had left for her, something that had belonged to her papa when he was in college. She wondered what it could be, and why her papa's college friend wanted her to have it. She would be glad to finally have the chance to open it.

Eiko knew there were going to be challenges ahead, but she had incredible peace that God would guide her and love her through the coming days. She leaned back into her seat as the plane soared into the star-filled night sky.

I see clearly now.
Sky blue remains in my heart.
The Son shines brightly.

Don't Miss the Other Books
in the Sky Blue Trilogy!

Clouds Gray: Eiko's dream of living on her own in Tokyo has been a dream come true. The bright lights and big-city atmosphere make her feel more at home with who she is as a person. At twenty-two years old, she is grateful for her small, but convenient apartment, her bustling workplace environment, and the close friends she has made.

But after the recent death of her beloved papa, Eiko has mixed emotions as she prepares to return home to Sapporo for the New Year's holiday. She prays the time spent together with her mother and brother will bring healing and hope. Eiko has discovered new life in Christ and radiates God's love. She longs to share the story of how she met the Lord and how much He means to her.

In *Clouds Gray*, Eiko encounters trials that test her new faith. Mother's emotional brokenness, her brother's personal problems, and the separation from her friends in Tokyo, including a special friend named Satoh, is weighing heavily on Eiko's heart and mind. But her most challenging trial is yet to come.

Will Eiko collapse under these stressful situations? Will she rise to overcome this dark, stormy season of her life? How will her relationship and life with Christ help her?

Bamboo Green: Twenty-two year old Eiko has emerged from a difficult season of physical, emotional, and spiritual trials with a stronger spirit and deeper relationship with Jesus Christ. With a positive attitude and a loving support group, Eiko contemplates her future, living and working in Tokyo.

One day, alone in a beautiful park, Eiko recalls the story of the bamboo plant. Even with no visible sign of growth for five years, a bamboo seed needs to be watered faithfully because unseen growth is taking place underground. A strong root system is forming to provide the foundation for the rapid growth that will follow, making the bamboo plant difficult to destroy. Bamboo can reach its full height and diameter in the first season. Branches and leaves form through additional seasons, as bamboo forests mature and flourish.

As the sun shines on her face, Eiko hears the Lord whisper to her, "Eiko, you are like a bamboo plant. You will mature quickly if you continue to follow Me, and I will use you to bless others." Eiko bows her head and weeps.

Bamboo Green, the third book in the Sky Blue Trilogy, follows Eiko's family, friends, and acquaintances, as she shares His love in Japan and beyond.

LIST OF JAPANESE WORDS AND ENGLISH MEANINGS

aa, Shu yo!: a desperate cry out to the Lord, asking for His intervention in a troubled time

arigatou gozaimasu: formal thank you

arigatou: thank you

Baputesuto kyoukai: Baptist church

chan: an informal title for females that goes after the person's name; includes, but not limited to, female family members, children, friends,

daijoubu: safe, secure, all right

dosanko: those born in Hokkaido

douzo: please, by all means

genkan: entryway

genki: in good spirits, cheerful, energetic

gohan: cooked rice/special meal with rice as the main ingredient

gyouza: Japanese pot stickers

hai, sou desu: yes, that is so

hai: yes

ikebana: the art of Japanese flower arrangement

itadakimasu: said in unison before meals to show gratitude for the food, also a signal to start eating

juku: cram school, after regular school hours

kanji: a system of Japanese writing using Chinese characters

konbanwa, minna san: good evening, everyone

konnichiwa: good afternoon

kun: an informal title for males, placed at the end of the person's name; includes, but not limited to, boys or juniors at work, and males of the same age and status to each other.

mikans: easy-peeling Japanese citrus, similar to tangerines

miso: traditional Japanese soup, consisting of a stock called "dashi," boiled, dried kelp (seaweed) and dried bonito (fish), into which softened miso paste is mixed. Other seasonal ingredients can be added.

moshi moshi: telephone greeting, meaning "Hello. Are you there?

nihonbare: sky blue; glorious, ideal weather, thought by Japanese to be unique to Japan. The clear sky and sun remind Japanese of their national flag.

norimaki: "rolled sushi" with sushi rice and sushi ingredients, wrapped in dried seaweed with a filling of vegetables, fish, or both in the center, which is beautifully displayed in the 3-centimeter cut pieces.

obentou: lunchbox

ocha: green tea

ofuro: Japanese soaking bath, filled with deep, hot water that covers your body; it requires soaping up and rinsing off outside the tub before entering.

ohayou gozaimasu: good morning

oishii: delicious

onigiri: Japanese rice balls formed into a triangular shape and often wrapped in seaweed

osembe: Japanese rice crackers with various flavors

oyakodon: chicken and egg, simmered together in a sauce and then served on top of a large bowl of rice

samurai: the warriors of pre-modern Japan

san: honorific title, which goes after the person's name (i.e., Sakamoto san.)

tatami: a type of rice mat, used as flooring material in traditional Japanese-style rooms

tonkatsu: a breaded, deep-fried pork cutlet, often served with shredded cabbage

zabuton: floor cushion

A Recipe for Japanese Curry Rice from the Author, Karol Whaley

An easy, satisfying dish, this recipe serves three to four people. It may be doubled or tripled for large groups.

SHOPPING LIST

1. Japanese Rice: Buy a small bag of Boton Brand Calrose Rice, available at stores in USA. Follow the directions to make two cups of rice, or use a rice cooker. Minute rice should not be used.
2. Buy a 3.5 oz. (100 grams) box of instant curry blocks from the S&B Golden Curry brand or from House Foods Vermont Curry, available at local supermarkets. Choose your level of spiciness—mild, medium, or hot.
3. Additional Ingredients
   One pound boneless, skinless chicken
   One small bag of baby carrots
   One medium potato
   One small onion
   Vegetable oil (2 and ½ TBSP)
   Ketchup (1 TBSP)

COOKING INSTRUCTIONS

Chop the chicken and peeled potatoes into ½ inch bite-sized cubes. Slice ½ cup of baby carrots. Boil them together in water with 1 TBSP of vegetable oil in a pan on the stove until tender. Check on them several times. Drain with the lid when they are ready. Return to the pan.

Take out a frying pan. Put in 1 and ½ TBSP of oil in the bottom of the pan. Remove the instant curry blocks from the box and place them, one by one, in the pan. Add 2 and ½ cups of water, stirring continuously on medium heat until the mixture is blended and becomes thicker. Put in ¼ cup of chopped onions for a few minutes. Turn off the heat and add 1 TBSP ketchup to the curry sauce. Pour the sauce over the chicken and vegetables. Stir well. Keep warm until served.

TO SERVE:

Put a scoop of cooked rice into one-half of a bowl or plate, and a ladle of curry onto the other half. Eat with a large spoon.

This recipe can be customized in many ways. It can also be made with beef or pork. The amounts of each ingredient can be changed to personal preferences. The microwave can also be used to cook the meat and vegetables. The Japanese love to garnish this dish with Benishoga, which is bright red pickled, shredded ginger (available at Asian markets), but it is also delicious without it. Enjoy!

Acknowledgments

There are several people I wish to thank who helped *Sky Blue* reach this point.

Thanks to my husband, Tom, and our two children, Joy and Jeremy, who shared the experience of living in Japan with us and for their encouragement for this project. Also, to their spouses, Matt and Amanda, who visited Japan, and to our five sweet grandchildren who love to hear stories and learn about Japan.

I am grateful to the Lord for the many wonderful Japanese friends and acquaintances He brought into our lives, who were so kind to share not only their culture but also their hearts with us through the years. You blessed us in so many ways and will always remain close in our hearts.

I also want to acknowledge all of the individuals and churches in the USA who felt burdened to pray for us as we learned to adjust to a culture very different from our own and a difficult new language. We felt your prayers and saw God at work in our lives.

Sky Blue is a work of fiction. Each one of the characters—their names and characteristics—are the product of my imagination and took on a life of their own as the story unfolded. I owe a debt of gratitude to Kathi Macias, who edited *Sky Blue*, as well as Jim Hart with Hartline Literary Agency, who found a path to publication.

My prayer for you, the reader, is that you will know that you, too, are precious to the Lord.

About the Author

Karol Whaley and her husband lived as Christian workers in Japan for over two decades. The Sky Blue trilogy is a work of fiction but embodies Karol's love for Christ and for the Japanese people. She and her husband, their children and grandchildren, live in southern California.

Karol hopes that you will also enjoy reading *Clouds Gray*, coming out soon, and the final book, *Bamboo Green*, by the end of the year. She can be contacted at jkotoba@aol.com.

IF YOU LIKED THIS BOOK, YOU MIGHT ALSO LIKE THESE BOOKS FROM OTHER HARTLINE/WHITE GLOVE AUTHORS:

A Heart's Gift by **Lena Nelson Dooley:** Because of an earlier betrayal, Franklin vows never to open his heart to another woman. But he desires an heir. When Lorinda is finally out from under the control of men who made all the decisions in her life, she promises herself she will never allow a man to control her again. But how can she provide for her infant son? Marriage seems like the perfect arrangement until two people from Franklin's past endanger Lorinda. How can he save her? And how will this affect the way they feel about each other?

Christine's Promise by **Kay Moser:** Christine Boyd is the envy of all the ladies in Riverford, Texas, in 1885. She is, after all, the daughter of a revered Confederate general and the wife of a wealthy banker, Richard Boyd. Beautiful, accomplished, elegant—she exhibits the exquisite manners she was taught in antebellum Charleston. She is the perfect southern lady. Or is she? The truth is that Christine's genteel outward demeanor hides a revolutionary spirit. When she was ten years old and fleeing Union-invaded Charleston, she made a radical promise to God. She plans to keep that promise. Tradition-bound Riverford, Texas, may never be the same.

***His Pepper Heart* by Brandy Heinamen:** Their date was entirely forgettable. The meal maxed out the spicy scale; the conversation, not so much. If she hadn't stolen Zachary's journal–or read the stupid thing–she never would've fallen for him. Fessing up is unpalatable, but unless she returns the journal, how will she have a prayer of seeing her name peppered across its pages? This quirky romance is a snack-sized story that satisfies. More than foodie fiction—it's a literary small plate, loaded with savory scenes and a long finish that lingers well after the characters have left the table.

***The Moses Conspiracy* by Susan Reinhardt:** A trip to post-terrorized Washington, D.C., in 2025 and a buggy accident in Bird-in-Hand, PA, set in motion events that expose a diabolical plan to destroy the Christian community. Ellie and John Zimmerman find themselves embroiled in a life-threatening investigation, fighting a shadowy enemy. Convinced it's now safe to visit D.C., Ellie and her 8-year-old son, Peter, travel to the nation's capital. But troubles erupt for her and Peter there and for her husband John at home as well. People are getting hurt, and their own family receives ominous warnings. Turning back the clock is not an option. Caught between strained family relationships and a faceless enemy, the couple rely on God for wisdom and protection. While they may expose the culprits, will they survive the heartache it brings?

The Rogue's Daughter **by Molly Noble Bull:** Had she really stood in front of God and church and minister, and allowed herself to be joined to Seth Matthews for life? In 1890 and a short time after graduating from a college for teachers in San Antonio, Texas, Rebecca Roberts found herself with both the teaching job she desperately needed and something else she had been determined never to have—a husband. Seth Matthews, a rugged, independent widower, had hired Rebecca to teach his three children, then married her "to save her reputation." It was a legal arrangement only, no love involved. Or was there? The azure skies, sun-baked earth, and majestic live oaks of Seth's south Texas ranch afford the setting for the most important lessons of this story. Rebecca learns about trust and tenderness, and Seth learns about the God she loves.